# THE SOAPBOX

Phillip Edmonds was the co-managing editor of *Wet Ink: the magazine of new writing* between 2005 and 2012. In 1997 he completed his PhD on the contemporary short story in Australia. He has lectured in Australian Literature and Creative Writing at the University of Adelaide, Griffith University and the Victorian College of the Arts.

***Acknowledgements for previous publication***

'The Soapbox', *Griffith Review*, autumn, 2008.

'The Trip', *Confessions & Memoirs: Best Stories under the Sun*, Central Queensland University Press, 2006.

'Missing out on Indy', *Best Stories under the Sun*, Central Queensland University Press, 2004.

'Foxes', *Vignette Press* Mini Shots, Melbourne, 2008.

'By the Grace of God', *Mattoid*, 1996.

***Also by Phillip Edmonds***

*Big Boys* (short stories), Second Back Row Press, 1979.

*Don't Let Me Fall* (short stories), Red Hill Press, 1991.

*Leaving Home with Henry* (novella), Arcadia/Australian Scholarly Publishing, 2010.

*Tilting at Windmills: the literary magazine in Australia 1968–2012*, University of Adelaide Press, 2015.

# THE SOAPBOX

PHILLIP EDMONDS

Arcadia

First published 2018 by ARCADIA

*the general books' imprint of*

Australian Scholarly Publishing Pty Ltd

7 Lt Lothian St Nth, North Melbourne, Vic 3051

Tel: 03 9329 6963 / Fax: 03 9329 5452

enquiry@scholarly.info / www.scholarly.info

ISBN 978-1-925801-20-0



*Cover design* Amelia Walker

*for Bruce Murray*

'To live means to finesse the processes to which one is subjugated.'

Bertolt Brecht, *On Politics and Society*

# CONTENTS

# THE SOAPBOX

Warwick loved his soapbox because standing on it he'd become the centre of attention for once, especially when he convinced his friends to come around and listen between games of cricket down the front drive. They didn't seem to understand much of what he said, but they were politely amused for time enough to have a lunch break.

The rough sides were smashed together with a few of Dad's biggest roofing nails. It had little steps, parts of which had once been bits of Mum's old stepladder that she'd used to get up to the top kitchen cupboard so as to clean out any unwanted groceries and pickle jars. His mother dozed off in the afternoons and wouldn't listen to him, but when she did, she displayed anger because she was frightened for him and said, to his frustration, 'Don't you get on your soapbox with me my boy.'

Warwick Moss always believed in democracy and that hadn't changed now that he was in England. As a boy in Australia he'd jump up and down about the evil in the world and avidly read the newspaper in the morning so he wouldn't feel empty, unfulfilled, with nothing much to think about. His family said his obsessions were stupid, unnecessary and impractical. They felt that they couldn't afford him, because there wasn't much money and because no one had ever seriously listened to them. In England, he imagined, there would be a more eccentric idea about speaking out, and if one made a success of it, you could be at the centre of something, instead of seeing your words evaporating across a silent landscape.

At school he was an 'intellectual', a small boy with serious intentions, in a rough state high school. And because no one wanted to listen to him, he built his own soapbox out of old fruit boxes and put it up in the corner of the backyard, next to the vegetable patch. From it he rehearsed his speeches and conducted the Melbourne Symphony Orchestra with a knife and fork.

School was tedious until first period in Year Twelve when Mrs May sat in front of the history class, behind a pile of books. She told them that they'd be studying stories, the people who told them and why, and in whose interests. She loved the historian Manning Clark, she said, because he spoke about Australian settlement in epic stories of good and evil, weakness and strength. And there was an Economics teacher who taught Warwick things he already knew when he watched his father come home tired and dispirited from work every day; that if you had no assets you'd become like the working class who lived in slums; that his family never had as much money as their rich relatives and there were people who could break you if you weren't subservient. Still, he persisted in believing free speech might make things fairer.

When he arrived for the first time at university the sight of the thousands of books in the huge library was too much to bear. He just wanted to know everything, and he could never understand why other people didn't feel the same. He just loved those piles of useless knowledge.

From England he remembered that time as a cicada summer during which the Labor party had lost another election because it opposed the war in Vietnam. In 1966 its leader Arthur Calwell was nearly assassinated by a man who said he wanted to be somebody and became it for a week or two. Yet there was a careless air, as if anything was possible, and underneath a feeling that 'democracy' was, of course, only a partial story – that some people owned it (like most other things), and taking things seriously was as stupid as running in the heat or getting upset because, Australians did not have foolish passions. The migrants were like that, his father would have said – you know the Greeks and the Italians – rather emotional – lovely people, but much of what they did was uncalled for.

Warwick wondered whether there was a place in Australia like Europe – where there was so much history there was sorrow in the stones. He had looked for European democracy in *National Geographic* magazines, but he couldn't find it except in photos. Democracy in Australia was as elusive as spinifex bushes in a long flat place such as the Mallee. Europe, the home of the great philosophers, certainly wasn't a place where the next big thing was a wheat silo in a heat haze on the horizon, or the promise of a thin line of trees where there could be a creek, a sign of promise out of nowhere.

* * *

In London he was working for the Ministry for the Arts in a great stone edifice near Whitehall. They liked him at the interview because they said Australians, although sometimes abrasive, make things happen.

'They work hard, like Rupert Murdoch', the personnel officer Sally said, fingering a glass paperweight, her lips perfectly framing the words. Warwick watched her, careful that his awareness could be making her a cliché.

'We want a project officer to take responsibility for the public speaking forums under our jurisdiction', she explained, almost quietly. 'Your experience in community arts in Australia will be most useful. We are looking for someone who is passionate about western democracy – that it operates at grass roots levels and is seen to be vibrant.'

After she finished speaking, the details of their meeting faded in a great sweep, like the time, years ago when he had driven into the Mallee looking for cultural opportunities that could be cultivated. It had been hot, and thoughts (if you could call them that) melted like daydreams. But on this day in London he concentrated on the position statement. The '90s had done that much to the brain, he thought. The 'position', Sally said (he noted how interesting it was that she didn't say 'job', in the way blunt Australians might), 'is to facilitate and service our range of performers at the Speakers Corner in Hyde Park'.

'You may be aware that in recent years the number of voluntary speakers at Hyde Park have been dwindling, perhaps due to people getting older and the Internet, among other cultural factors', Sally said, delicately moving her reading glasses from her forehead onto the table in front of her.

Warwick felt envious of Sally's assurance, her peachy cream complexion. When he was drawn into conversation with her, he heard himself sounding rough. Sally framed perfect sentences before she began to speak: 'The government feels that it has a responsibility to both our local constituency and the increasing number of tourists who have come to regard Speakers Corner as an icon, an essential part of London's cultural landscape.' With that and some discussion about salary, he had the job.

Warwick lived in Hampstead, in a house leafy enough to be spacious, which gave them the anticipation of dreaming of backyards, but raffish enough to bring forth the knowledge that London is full of desperate people who have little style to speak of. Warwick was glad of the job. His Masters in Politics hadn't brought him very much other than the heartache of knowing that he knew so little, and desired too much, and he was jealous of academics who had assembled a body of books. Yet the ones he knew seemed tired, especially in London, because no one could ever claim they were making a New World.

Warwick found out on his first day on the job that the previous cultural development officer had been a dud, a Cambridge trained man who'd been too stiff and inflexible and he had little idea of how to motivate his speakers, let alone hold them.

Hyde Park Speakers Corner was a relic, its list of professional speakers reduced to one Pentecostal and two animal liberationists. If it hadn't been for the Japanese tourist buses that followed the city guide brochures printed by the Ministry of the Environment, it would have been forgotten years ago.

He remembered Maggie Thatcher's words about there being no society, only self-interest, and his predecessor believed volunteering was the sort of thing people did when they went on hunt club rosters or had discreet games of sub-county cricket. But he was going to set up a series of paid speakers who could talk about anything, so it was out with a refined volunteerism promoted by chaps and in with some aggressive marketing from a flaxen-haired Antipodean.

* * *

The speakers hadn't been turning up – it wasn't the weather, even though in typical English style it had been lousy. The passionate Trotskyite, became an evangelical Christian preacher in Manchester, and the only knowledgeable Marxist went off and became a Mathematics teacher on the internet. People said it was the new technologies that had replaced face-to-face storytelling, and whereas once a place like Speaker's Corner could be said to be quaint, there were other cute places to contend with.

Perhaps the problem was that there wasn't an actual meeting place in the park: a raised symbol of some description, a platform (like his old soapbox) that people could at least reject. He desperately wanted to imagine that there could be a boundless electronic community unencumbered by narrow gossip.

You can have opinions on the internet in private, he decided. All the smart people were chatting on the internet so he advertised on his web site the highlights of the ensuing week, but the crowds weren't any more than twenty people on a good day.

On another windy wet afternoon in Hyde Park, as usual Warwick made position under the fattest oak tree next to the entrance at the gate. Past him, the traffic on Pall Mall streamed past, every second car a squat black taxi, their occupants barely visible as they sped off into a city of a million laneways and destinations. He realised, for once, that he really didn't have his heart in the project. His blunt assertiveness (which he'd often thought of as charming) wasn't working well enough. Somehow, he'd managed to increase the number of speakers from the meagre assortment he'd inherited when he'd first taken over to about fifteen, but it was the usual suspects who covered a cross section of opinions and positions, a template for his old ideas about 'democracy'.

Whenever Warwick raised his concerns with Sally, she was, it seemed, blissfully confident that he would rescue the old English institution. He told her that he didn't think that he was being in any way successful, but she waved it away with an aristocratic swish of her delicately preserved English arm. He was attracted to Sally for all the reasons he detested himself. She was a stand-out from the pack, like the spires of Oxford and of exquisite, secret places that would never become ordinary and every day.

The speakers were quite cheap because their payment was a commission on top of their dole. Mostly, they were recent graduates of some of the better red brick universities, and to add some difference he'd managed to attract a fair sprinkling of mature-age characters who added a more modulated and earnest tone to what Sally kept calling 'the event'.

Failure didn't seem to upset Sally at all, he imagined, because she'd just go home to the family seat in Shropshire where the library was lined with so many classics it didn't matter all that much whether there wasn't a clear future because the past was so inspiring and comfortable.

They had, of course, been seeing each other – to use one of those cool expressions of the late 1990s, in between meetings for polite, seductive conversations, and after hours for 'the sex', as people called it. He was a poor bugger, because he thought of it as making love; it seemed a better way to sum up his feelings but she laughed and he realised just how powerless most men were in the face of such beauty. 'We are physically attracted to each other', she announced matter-of-factly. Australia, he thought, had made him practical, even utilitarian to the extent that sex at home had been more like a job of work. But in England, the avenues for foreplay were classicr, more restrained (hidden away), and her soft skin was a glorious canvas, which he was allowed to caress and then add to with the flick of her hair from a shoulder that harder men than him would die for. The sex was good, because they'd never spend enough time together to bore each other, and she would leave for Shropshire, and he'd eventually go home to Australia, to a flat place of some description. To be fair to her, he had some kind of power as he gazed at her extraordinary figure, her manicured hands and fantasised that he could consume her.

The speakers tried hard enough. They were erudite and well-read and really quite amusing. But week by week, the number of people (other than the Japanese on the tour buses), who stopped to listen other than to walk their dogs or jog around the running track on the perimeter of the park wasn't any more than a hundred or so hardy souls. There was even an absence of healthy heckling.

Warwick became irritable and began to notice that ordinary English people, other than comedians and politicians, weren't really very funny, which was uncharitable of him, so he felt like quitting as he pined for dry Australian jokes and people who'd make Hyde Park funny for a few hours. Instead, there was only a collection of bag ladies and gaunt druggies trying to cadge coins.

He'd warned Sally that he'd soon quit, but she giggled again and only invited him out for tea. So on the Friday before the last Sunday of June, in fine weather (so there weren't any excuses for poor attendance), he cancelled all of his speakers with one definitive email written in plain language in a gesture that was an extreme move and a plaintive plea. He needed to try out something new and, due to the state of things in our democracies, silence might just be the best thing.

She did say, though, that he was a disappointment, and someone who never struck her as a quitter – that the job wasn't under threat due to funding cuts in the civil service and that, 'in any case, the important thing was that things be seen to be done as much as being done.'

Warwick wondered whether his brother in Australia could remember how the old soapbox had been built, because when they became teenagers it had become embarrassing to behold out in the backyard. Sometimes, when it rained, they'd take it into the shed, but it was wonky by then, and out of shape, and a construction of children you should have known better. It was rough, of a type suggesting that anything much will do. If only he had put as much time into its construction as into his best speeches. He phoned his brother Peter, who said he remembered how it went and that he'd send the details in an email attachment the next day. In Melbourne Peter drew it as best he could, wonky bits and all. That brother of his was a stupid bugger, he thought. What on earth could he want it for?

Rebuilding it would be hard because in a place like England he was never sure that people kept any old junk, particularly in London where the upper middle class predominated. Their lives seemed dedicated to the elimination of mess, and good old useful junk was a working-class trait, and if there was any, it could only be found somewhere remote. It was bloody embarrassing hawking around London for relics, so he rang one of his ex – speakers who was a carpenter during the daytime – a relic in his own right, a master craftsman turning out beautiful furniture for clients with no taste. Harry said he could make it 'big enough to stand on and small enough to be polite'.

* * *

There was only silence at Speakers Corner except for a few tramps wondering whether it was a public holiday from speaking. The tour buses arrived on cue, disgorging tourists who behaved as if there was still something to see, but being polite and Japanese they used their videos so they wouldn't waste their film. It took two weeks to build the soapbox, during which time Warwick resigned from the Ministry and Sally told him that their relationship had concluded and was just no longer appropriate.

Harry made the soapbox the way Warwick imagined it, even allowing for the distortion of time and the fact that there weren't any black and white photos to go by. And Warwick performed his last act as Cultural Development Officer, Class 2 for the Ministry for the Arts by digging some foundations in the park before dawn while Harry had it fitted just right so it would hold to the new cement. By dawn they had it complete with the addition (for local conditions) of a steel grill and a sign, 'Anyone speaking on this construction will be prosecuted.' It was brown and glorious in the early light, with little steps at the side in case anyone wanted to climb up and speak.

The funny thing was that, over the next few weeks, even after the structure was removed by some council workers, there were reports of crowds returning to the place where the soapbox had been, marked only by the cement slab and sheered-off bolts. The Japanese tourists arrived, videoed the bolts and listened to the story of the soapbox told by one of the tramps who claimed that it was a Western equivalent of a temple that had been too fragile to be left unattended.

But people also said they heard the beginnings of some great stories and at least one inspiring speaker – real stories in the park instead of relics told in transparent tones. The crowds were made up of people who talked to each other every day of their lives; it just was that no one had made them famous for something as ordinary as breathing.

Sally hadn't really cared if the whole Hyde Park venture failed. 'That kind of success was such a silly idea anyway. When will you people realise that we create these things to keep you entertained?' she had announced the last time she saw him. Warwick, for his part, realised that he'd be better working in a boring place like home, where he might never be important. He stopped stressing about whether anyone was listening and gave up on being ashamed of daring to dream.

# THE GREEN VALIANT

Dad decided that we needed to go up in the world so he bought a new Chrysler Valiant. It came home one night at about six o'clock. We always watched cars going up and down the hill outside, the school bus with snow on the roof one winter, and I remember next door's billycarts careering into Mum's azaleas, but when the Valiant came, I must say, we went up in the world.

It was green, emerald green, very American, stylish and modern unlike us. The Carters only had the latest Ford Falcon, it was blue and white with hard seats, but our Valiant was wonderful because it had stitched seats that seemed to be like muscular pillows.

The Valiant had curves and riding in it we felt like film stars especially as Dad would parade around the shops pretending to look for a parking spot and we'd wave at the Browns as they struggled back from the shops in their old Holden.

Dad had always wanted to move up in the world. After twenty years in the firm he'd become the state manager and the days of overalls and grimy singlets were gone. He had suits and ties and needed a car to complement such a new life. The best thing about the Valiant was the big boot with the fake spare tyre imprint sticking out the back. There was a mahogany dashboard with white buttons that went in and out according to weather conditions and lighting considerations, a demister that took away any frosted breath, and farting (according to Mum), whose job it was to keep us in order on long trips.

Getting back to the curves: they made us feel special as we lived our lives in straight lines under the Liberals, four streets from the train station, up from the shops, frightened that we'd be invaded by Asians and other complete strangers. But the Americans and Chrysler Valiants were ok. I think it was because we felt small in some way. And we were small. My brother and I played with the Thomas boys, Warren and Tom, who were older than us, in our sand pit out the back, or down the creek chasing rats.

We felt that big things happened in England or America, except when the Japanese bombed Darwin, but that was in Dad's time and he often told us about it. He'd been injured in New Guinea you see, just when the Prime Minister said we'd make our last stand where Brisbane is, if the tropical parts fell to the Asians. The point was that we didn't know anything much about them as we rode around in the green Valiant. Asians were a different colour and we had black and white TV, so it was no wonder that that car stood out in the street.

American ice creams also came to us. Dad's idea of a posh outing was when we went down to the shops and bought liquorice, strawberry and lemon striped vanilla in cones. The green Valiant was glorious and garish in the late afternoon light. My sister, even though never melodramatic, thought she was in a movie, which was a pity because she only married a bloke from the church. We had a rich uncle you see, he'd been the one who'd introduced us to the ice creams, and even though the Valiant was great to ride in, I really think that dad had got an American car to impress him. We'd moved up in the world and the challenge would be the next time we drove to Sydney to show them what was what.

So we went to Sydney up the old Hume Highway – it was windy and dangerous in places, but there was a minor hitch at the start. When we got to Pentridge Prison at Coburg (where opponents of the Vietnam War would later be locked up), Mum discovered that we'd left the beach umbrella at home, se we had to go back. Sydney you see was a place of sun and sophistication to Melbournians then. You drove up there in more ways than one.

The trip was really boring to my brothers but I liked it because in those days the Automobile Association published strip maps that had minute details of the road between towns, little stories about how a place got its name and so forth. There was a 'Hopeless Creek' just outside Wangaratta that marked a dry creek bed and the spot where Hume and Hovell became desperate for a time, a bunyip lagoon where the mythical animal got washed up in a flood. The road went through the towns then, but they have been bypassed now. Our green Valiant purred past creaky trucks and ordinary people towing trailers.

On past trips we'd always stay the first night in Albury and this time, even though we were much faster and we got there early, the motel man was most impressed with our new acquisition as he wryly suggested that we might need a bigger parking space as he ushered us in. I can't recall all of it of course, and to do that would disturb the truth, but we passed the milestone of Yass, where older cars usually died from exhaustion, you'd see them piled up like tin cans in wreckers' yards – graveyards to when distance dominated us even more.

Dad said that he would give us a lolly for every green Valiant we could spot on the final ride into Sydney. Somewhere he'd hidden a bag of them in the fake mahogany glove box. We looked and looked and even as the traffic built up outside the Canberra turnoff there wasn't one to be seen. No American cars anywhere at all and I thought that there might be some coming out of Canberra seeing that our government loved their foreign policy so much. A huge Ford Custom line came at us from the direction of Goulburn though. As we got closer to Sydney there was one! A green one, a couple of cars in front on a long flat stretch of road and the people in the Morris Minor just in front of us looked envious and very small with their windows down as they craned to catch a glimpse of us as we sailed past intent on conquering the rest of the world.

Sydney was always busy. Green double decker buses swayed as they cornered, drinkers sat on the pavement outside pubs to escape the heat, but we had moved up in the world. The thing we had to do though was find our Uncle's place on the North Shore over the bridge. As we glided across the span, looking down on the blue of the harbour, I'm sure I saw a glimpse of America, even that far across the Pacific. It was how the mind plays tricks, or how the imagination makes up the truth. Either way, it was there.

As we motored up the main road out of North Sydney and then parked outside our rich Uncle's place, dad had an epiphany. We saw another green Valiant across the street; they seemed to be multiplying around us. We of course were looking for them by then, as we moved up in the world. Dad saw himself suddenly as someone who was different then, after he had even driven all that way in a suit. And it wasn't long before I also saw how we had changed.

It was ten years later, long after we'd returned to Melbourne down the lonely highway, past the stoic sheep and bemused horses. I remember, as clearly as if it were yesterday, the way things built up into a seductive pattern we happily participated in. We wanted to be like rich Americans, to be driven and move up in the world. Then, it became all too clear. Warren Thomas, who had been in the senior grade at school, and been our playmate, went to the Vietnam War and never came home.

# THE TRIP

Mum told me she wanted to go on a trip. 'To where?' I inquired kindly. She was sitting up at last, instead of slumping back against the pillows with a far-away look in her eyes, or getting caught up again in her blankets. I'd come off the street. It had been a day for business in the city, of making sure the arrangements were just right: where the money would go and of visiting clean funeral parlours where nice gentlemen nodded and nudged you into considering coffins.

It was a nice enough room in a more than adequate hospital, with a Greek grandmother in the next bed who admitted streams of sons with their quiet little daughters into her huge hugs. She'd go with a bang, I first thought, and then I knew it would be some kind of soliloquy full of little sounds, and, in the background, a steady wailing like it is in the bush late at night, when animals call to one another. There would be black, lots of it like in Zorba, but it wouldn't be like that for my mum, because as Protestants we'd go to our church down careful paths, trying to look cheery. But the kids would cry, and then, at last, after such a long trip, we wouldn't be able to contain it any longer, and we would let go in case it cut us in half. Self-preservation is very strong with us.

Outside, across the lawn, there were sensible shrubs and a few wattle trees. It must have been late winter or maybe early spring for they were yellow, blowing about in wind, which refused to go away. The hospital was on one of those gentle hills in Camberwell from where you can see the city skyline thrusting away in a type of mock permanence. The walls were a clean blue-grey on which pastoral scenes were captured behind glass, and the nurses came up to you and told you things, because, I suppose, you looked as though you cared, with what could commonly be called a relative emotional involvement.

I bought her some chocolates – soft centres, which she devoured like a monkey with thin fingers grabbing around among the cute brown wrappers. Someone else had the same idea because there were quite a few boxes, so we gorged ourselves in what I now see as our last flurry of domesticity. She noticed that my pants had a hole in them, so she insisted on finding a needle and thread, but of course we couldn't find one, even though we tried to, but Janine the charge sister was very understanding when it came to Alzheimer's patients. 'They are always doing that kind of thing dear', she told me later when Mum had gone to the toilet to cough up blood and relieve her bruised bowels. But she was smiling – you see – some of the Greeks gave her a hand. One little girl, in fact, carried Mum's handbag, and was polite and didn't think it strange that a sick old lady would want it with her in the toilet.

By the time she got back, the bed was covered in brown wrappers. I hadn't been able to contain myself – those soft centres were so seductive and comforting as I'd anxiously perused them by fingering their moulded shapes. How the cream trickled after a bit of sucking from the shell. I'd gone back to our backyard – my brother and I setting up soldiers in the dirt under the apricot tree next to the rhubarb patch, the budgies chirping maniacally in their aviary. But I seemed now too tall for the trenches and the train set refused to go and there was dirt and hair in the wind-up parts. The carriages had gone.

Still, she insisted on mending the pants and Janine and I was tired of talking about them, and it was of course kind of embarrassing because the hole was near my inner leg. But the Greeks were really nice and even looked at it in case they could help. I like Greeks I concluded, even the ones who had planted fennel in the backyard at Northcote, which wouldn't ever come out, even with a mattock. They want to be kind, and expect kindness in return. They are kind of co-operative, unlike us.

Anyway, Mum couldn't comprehend that there weren't any chokies left so we scoured the ward for chocolate royals and anything that remotely looked like a scotch finger. Up the end, a wiry old bird gave us some Tim Tams. I'm wary of them because they seem to make me emotional – it could be the colouring: but we chomped along as though we had at last set out on a trip – had set in for the duration and needed something to relive the scenery.

She talked of Dad a lot with her mouth open and caramel dribbling down her jaw. 'He was a good man', she said. 'He has gone away now you know …' and then a pause as she trailed off. 'I want to tell you something,' she added. She was clear for what seemed like ten minutes – intent, bolt upright in concentration. 'I love you, you are a strange bird, but I love you …' and I stopped her and shushed her. Then she was away across the sea somewhere. 'We'll go to England,' she said strongly.

'Why England?' I asked. But there was no reply that had any prose to it. I had heard of the possible permutations of our family tree and found the possibilities imaginative. That maybe there was a relative in Cornwall, a windswept place where Druid armies travel cobbled roads at night. Maybe they were calling her – I didn't think it funny. Glen Iris to Cornwall, now that had a sophisticated ring to it! She had been there once with Dad; an ANZ Bank European excursion, which ended up in the mother country. A bus in Paris hit him, but that's another story. Back in England he drove her around the counties in a Cortina from one of the hire companies, and, in her words, he didn't stop at the more interesting places and insisted on only driving along roads that had signs.

'Do you believe in God?' she asked me, and I wished that the nurse would pop around the alcove and save me.

'Well, yes, sort of . . .' I said. She wanted to know if I had an answer, and it was urgent I supposed because this could be the last time we had a chat. I fiddled again at the hole, which hardly helped, for it only caught her eye. 'I do,' I said softly in case too many people overheard us. 'Well then,' she said, 'we'll take him along with us on our trip.' I nodded reassuredly. She was getting excited. The blankets were all caught up again in her feet. She was insisting that she must get packed. It was a long way to England and she would need lots of clean pants, a warm coat and her handbag. But we calmed her down, as they say. I had to go, not for any reason in particular – it was just by then I knew we had been there and white graceful birds were circling in an up draught of our own making.

# FOXES

Last night I heard a stranger, an animal moving about in the light scrub just outside the back door, the door I'd locked in case something feral came in. My fears began last year in the drought when there'd been a rat in the rafters and mice running all over the kitchen. I got up and spoke softly to it in case it wished to stay, but I startled it and it moved away like a kangaroo.

Forty years ago *he* heard similar sounds on their first night in the old house next to the creek. His wife Greta had made the evening meal using ingredients some might construe as German. Her English was faulty when she went shopping, but the locals said her money was as good as theirs, and that she shouldn't worry for, even though her countrymen had been defeated in the war, there was a place for them.

It was their first summer and the bright light lingered forever. Animal noises changed from bird-calls into discreet scurryings and long loping thuds and when it was hot *he* was lulled into believing that his estate outside Prague no longer existed. Here, instead, no one took an interest in anything much, but when he dreamt of his home country he saw green fields going on forever. There, no government had come anywhere near him except for one day when his tenants trooped up the hill with a red flag led by a student in spectacles. It was before the Germans came at the start of the war and he made sure he took down all their names.

But in the nearest town there was only gossip about what type of foreigner he could be, and how about he got there, seeing that his vowel sounds were so strange.

I'll tell you the story of this foreigner in this southern land and how I reminded him of the student in the spectacles because I too had come out of the city for reasons that were out of control.

You see, I was his nearest neighbour and one day when I was driving along our common track I hit his best dog as it jumped out from behind a bush. It lay still on the road with a smudge of blood behind its ear. He thought it was dead and I almost panicked because he had his gun and he wept like only a severely hurt man can. Tears streamed down his cheeks as he said over and over again, 'You have killed him, why didn't you stop.' It was the first words we'd exchanged in the three years I had been there. The dog didn't die because one night later on we ran across him in the dark searching for foxes.

That was where it all began. He and Greta had said to each other on the ship from Calais that no matter what happened they wouldn't live in a place that had politics.

'My homeland was destroyed during the war by politics', he told people, with an emphasis coming out of the corner of his mouth. They had had a migrant sponsor in central Victoria, a long way from the city and unions, he had explained to an elderly English lady on the ship out. He told her, 'We will grow things again; the communists took our land and called me names because I wanted to sell to the Germans during the war. We must survive you see.' The lady nodded.

'Yes, we have had the same problems in England—politics. There are too many people interested in politics. In Australia, you should have the chance to put that behind you as much as you can. You will like Australia, most Australians just mind their own business,' she replied.

All of this had remained unknown to the people of the district in so far as it was expressed in words, but everyone noted his silence and respected him for lacking passion.

He and Greta brought up their children in an old farmhouse and made a living from a chicken farm. In fact, there was so little talk that everyone had to make up their own snippets, that's if they cared enough on long winter days when the light was bad, for in summer it was too much of an effort. He sold his produce to men he thought very little of. He tolerated them in the way they tolerated him, in a business like way.

They had come to a place where ghosts stalked the entangled growth around their farm even though they had made it green, and every spring they made a special effort to cut the bush back. He rarely saw any foreign papers and it was only with sufferance that he read any of the local city editions. His brother wrote from Prague about the pitiful state of the worker's government and as for his old estate (as he feared) it had been divided up between peasant families 'who didn't care for it', he added at the foot of an aerogram. Such stories were relayed in an arrangement that was foreign, in a dialogue that belonged to no one anymore. And there were visitations day and night, sometimes along our common road. He said nothing to Greta, but she knew about the men on horseback in curvy helmets (with swords), who came when there was a high wind and who left traces in the dirt. But within a day of whatever weather, they were gone.

I tell you this story in this voice for he would not speak to me in a language that glimpsed at engagement, and because, I made him up just like he made me up. You see, despite the silence we were inseparable. I was his only neighbour past his place along an old disused track, which, went we went there, was covered in gauze.

* * *

*He* eyed our activities suspiciously. There were lots of birds, but rabbits and foxes predominated in such scarred and picked over country. He had to kill all the foxes because they taunted him by howling during the night and the smart ones got into his chickens. Some mornings he found broken eggs, feathers and carcases across his yard. The foxes, although cunning and not benign like the native animals, were lost spirits who scavenged along the edges of everyone else's world.

Their strangled cries came from the throat like a call that might never be answered. They were silent for much of the time, like the gypsies in the old country before the war, but under pressure they'd sing out. They were also handsome like the gypsies, and had beautiful tails, but they smelt.

He didn't say that when I found him with his gun in the bush one night trying to track their calls, but his face suggested that someone should keep them in order. He had his big male German shepherd on a leash and my dog sniffed at its buttocks by way of a suggested conversation, to no effect.

Every five years or so there was a drought. Crows picked at any ailing animal, and from a distance the top of the forest looked brown. It was coddling itself. At dusk we saw kangaroos struggling at the side of the dam and there weren't any young ones that season. Those crows, those stupid black birds became the only sound during the hot afternoons and he and I were in agreement. 'Shoot the bastards,' I'd mutter and mumble to myself and he heard me as he looked up from his burning off. Then a volley of shots rang out across the valley.

Because of his shooting the native animals were wary of getting too close. He had made it scary, and like a good neighbour, I said nothing because, after all, it was his business. The land was bigger than both of us. The rabbits weren't as fearful though, scurrying away at severe angles in front of oncoming vehicles, brazen imperialists running up and over the scarred hills. He had given up on them and was hoping all the while for an epidemic, some final solution that might make sense of their mess.

I think it was eight years ago when he started to talk more even though it wasn't a coherent story containing a past, and a childhood. It started when he stopped me one day on the road to complain about 'greenie hippies', as he put it, who were showing an interest in his property, which contained some old ruins.

'You know the village, where the Welsh were in the gold-rushes, when the mine worked?' he uttered. I'd heard Greta mention it once, her head down as she scurried away, mumbling something about how it should be left alone like they had been all these years. A foreign mining company wanted to look for gold in the hills behind his place. The hippies in the hills had heard reports of drilling rigs and men in land-cruisers trampling over the scarred land and drooling over the possibility of injecting the country with their equipment.

The town, and the country surrounding it, wasn't typical of other country places, but like anywhere, its meaning can be gauged by trying to work out the angles from where people speak. In our case, he and I were bound together by a common road, which went near their 'old place', as Greta called it.

The news of course leaked out, and like with most partly quaint and relatively dead things, archaeologists began poking about and groups of discreet tourists began visiting the part of the village that was on crown land. He owned half of it, he said, a group of stonewalls and some buildings protected under a giant blackberry bush. He didn't want all the attention. 'I don't want governments involved', he told me severely that day when he met me on the track, looking at me accusingly, for he knew that I was interested in the history of the valley, and where he came from was something he wouldn't talk about. Silence tried to cover everything and he insinuated that one thing led to another.

He went out shooting in the windy valley and brought home foxes in hessian bags. He dreamt again of men on horseback with curvy helmets, but he couldn't see their faces, and, unlike in the old country, he never knew the direction from which they galloped. He never told me that he thought the greenies looked wild and full of passion, and misguided love. And somewhere down our common track we heard the wailing of a woman, and the indiscriminate whimpering of lost, stillborn and murdered children.

Those greenies were a motley lot. We flee the city in more ways than one. But there were a couple of ex-communists who thought saving the old place was more than just a good idea. But, they loved politics, whereas the hippies thought politics encouraged aggression. In that way they were like him. They just wanted to be left alone.

Anyway, they finally won their battle by getting, as he'd put it, 'a government involved.' and for a brief time, there were tourists in the hills behind his place and he threatened to shoot them down like rabbits if they got out of control.

I'm sure he loved the place; it was just that he couldn't show it to anyone else in case he lost it, in the way he'd lost his place in Europe all those years ago, when he committed murder in the name of the family. 'For survival', he said.

‘Half of it is on private land you know, if I can’t have all of it then no one can have any of it’, he shouted at me. It was the last time we spoke and our exhausted syllables pounded and struggled with what might have been self-recognition. And it’s also true that I didn’t love enough when I was at that place. I’d been talking to myself for too long, but *he*, could never go home.

# MAGPIES

Jeff was rarely at home in the weatherboard house by the creek where he lived with a mate. Visitors remarked on the junk in the hallway and the assorted car parts on the porch, but he said he couldn't clean it all up because he was always away in other places doing more urgent things. For example, he was seeing a woman in Melbourne once or twice a week when he could get away from the radio station where he worked as a technician fixing all the things that broke down.

He'd met her in the local pub when she was up visiting a friend who worked at the primary school. Robin had been a primary teacher for nearly fifteen years, in a range of schools across the state.

She told her friend on that visit to town that Jeff intrigued her. He was like a fat boy she'd once had in grade three, who loved getting lollies for the teacher even if his desk was a mess and there were remnants of half eaten bananas in his schoolbag. But that boy was spirited and caring when it came to the other kids, she remembered. She told her friend that she could imagine making love with Jeff even though he wasn't an oil painting and sometimes talked of the 'emotional baggage' he carried around from his former wife. But, as she said, he was expansive and enthusiastic, unlike her *ex*. She was worried though about what he'd said about his dad, because you learn to trust such information when you are a teacher. How his childhood memories contained backyards of tractor tyres, impotent, greasy and rusty motor engines and clapped out refrigerators, all owned by his father who worked for the local water board repairing pipes and drains in preparation for the day when things might dry up.

She arranged for him to come to dinner the next time he was in the city. Jeff was really nervous, but he didn't show it and arrived at her place in Kensington the following week. Outside the flower shop in the main street he wavered between wanting to be caring and sophisticated or dorky and desperate.

He had thought of her often after that first meeting up country. Thought about some of the things she said, and what he imagined her legs were like. But he didn't go on with the latter, because it was, well a bit like treating a woman like an object, and he always said he wasn't a Freudian and too much in life was linked to sex. But there'd been a moment when he imagined Robin blushing in a way that linked her cheeks to her legs.

You know how animals circle each other at first meeting; we are the same. He gave her a book about a mythical woman in Mexican history who slept with Cortes the Spanish conqueror because it was about sex and power in less enlightened times. She took it in her delicate hand and he blushed and panicked because he thought that she might think he was suggesting something. She did, and admired him for what she hoped might be his intentions.

A different person would have parked their rusted old car around the corner, but Jeff didn't give it a second thought. She asked him into the living room. The house was very narrow and little light made it in.

In those days people paid fortunes for converted workers cottages so they could walk to a coffee shop. There was no room for exercise and if you had a gum tree out the back on hot days you could imagine it calling out to its brothers and sisters in places where they stretched out their branches.

Jeff had cleaned up a bit by ironing a white shirt and sponging down the front seat of his car. That night neither of them said much about where they'd been to get where they were, because to talk about emotional baggage on a first date is a bit off-putting, according to the women's magazines.

They continued to see one another by taking it in turns. One weekend she'd go to Ballarat, and then the next, he'd come down to Melbourne, always with presents, little things he'd found on his trips, useful trinkets and obscure first editions from second hand bookshops. He made some magnificent meals in her galley like kitchen looking out over the backyard that had become slightly more cluttered than when he first came into her life. He conducted obscure ingredients into a symphony of smells, steaming dishes constructed in a movement made only possible by men with ample stomachs and short arms – with flourishes of thick wrists and the certainty of bulk. And when he was finished (and they had eaten their fill), there was a sense of debt because she knew him to be a nice man, who cared for small things. But the kitchen was like a bombsite with bits of food everywhere and scores of dirty cooking utensils strewn along the benches. After such performances she watched him as he waited for her praise. But for a moment there was a false note in his orchestration when he mumbled that his ex-wife was too interested in cleaning to be romantic. 'She broke my heart', he said bitterly.

To do the dishes would have washed away the significance of the event like the time when he moved from a house in Carlton when everything became clean and he thought that no one would know that he'd been there and done good things.

It was years since Robin's *ex* had been in the house and the only thing of his left was a red lawnmower in the shed with which he'd tried to mow the back lawn on weekends after they separated. A way of maintaining contact, but it soon palled because all he got was a glass of lemonade after he finished. He had shovelled the clippings into neat piles, collected together the paperwork for the financial details of the property transfer into an expanding cardboard file and made it clear that he wasn't even thinking of anyone else even though she was bored with him.

Jeff stayed down one or two nights a week and joked about getting into her bed because there was the other man's absence in a bed side table with no photo albums and a space in the backroom where his boots used to be. He was considerate because as it stood she could be quite forthright and wanted him to pleasure her in ways that he would have found unimaginable on their first meeting. He was quite coy about being seen naked (and she wore sensible underwear), that came down to the top of her thighs and was held up by elastic just below her belly button. She became the sensual part of him, the body transformed in ways that made up for his lack of confidence.

Things started to go wrong when she got up sometime in the middle of the night to go to the toilet. Being a thin terrace house in Kensington the loo was still out the back in a little wooden outhouse. She'd always said that she wanted to fix up the inconvenience by getting in a plumber and a builder. Jeff offered to do the job, but as with a lot of things, he or she never got around to it, and the loo was a destination of some difficulty when visitors came.

It must have been two or three in the morning because there was no light from the sky and her bed-lamp was the only signpost. It all went wrong because Jeff left an old engine part (which he was going to install into Robin's ailing Mazda), in the hallway adjacent to the corner in the corridor leading to the kitchen. It was an oily, messy thing with bits of metal poking out of it; one of those things that made people think in daylight about the way the world worked and the price paid. Ultimately it was a grotty thing best left somewhere out of sight. But she tripped on it and at first she felt as if she had broken her leg. She returned to the bedroom and she could see the back of his big body under the blankets even in the darkness. He snored slightly in discontinuous bursts, and because he was sick his breath seemed like a series of optimistic gusts.

She didn't tell him how she had hurt herself, but she checked her leg under the lamp in case there was blood on her body. She decided that she'd wait until the morning to complain about how it happened, because it was just too hard to talk to anyone at that time.

He was always accommodating in ways that deflated her moments of concern. She felt that when she raised things she was being mean, even rude and he'd quake, go red and sometimes shake. But the sleeping figure harboured secrets such as how she'd look in suggestive underwear instead of the Bonds cottontails. He never raised his desire but it gnawed at him.

When they first met she charmed him through her organisational ability and the way in which the kitchen was stacked after shopping at the supermarket. She anxiously put things away in designated places and it amused him because he couldn't imagine doing anything like that. He watched her in different rooms of her house prioritising her possessions, making lists of useful things and what she could dispense with. Manageable piles of potential rubbish because she loved lists such as a long one on the fridge with highlighted sections in red and green texta colour coded combinations.

She kept thinking about earlier that night, how he had flamboyantly cooked for her in her cute kitchen, an elaborate four course meal, starting with a chunky pumpkin soup and then a huge marinated fish, concluded by a desert full of whipped cream, the latter all fluffy, high and elaborate. He had moved almost fluently, quite gracefully, because normally he clunked about in a pair of heavy brown boots, but on that night he was a big graceful bird, clutching onto kitchen implements as if they were conductor's batons. He moved quickly but his bulk prevented him from becoming chirpy. But the kitchen was a complete mess again with slops of disused food overflowing the sink and wiping down bench. Too much to even look at, discarded, stained dishes, piles of bottles which made her mad and the idea of eliminating the mess a torturous headache stretching forever. She appreciated the meal because her ex-husband Mick really wasn't interested in such things, but this man treated her like the cleaner.

He conversed on subjects he thought she cared about and listened intently with his hands close to his face and never folded in front of his chest like other males who felt they had to protect themselves. When they had sex he was relieved that he had got some of it, quite grateful that it seemed to have happened through magic. He'd been let into a place where he imagined someone else always had power.

Robin found though that the sex was nice because he was caring, if not masculine, in that he was overly anxious as to whether she was enjoying herself, so much so he kept asking her questions when they began to lose control. He was too conscious of his big belly and she was slim and curvy. He worried about how big his penis would look next to it so he sweated dissembled and stumbled, whereas, she pretty much wanted to get on with it because she concentrated hard and made the best of things. Somehow it worked (not like a seduction), instead, a performance of two people (led by one) who had decided exactly what she wanted. He was distant because of how worried he'd become, but she said she didn't mind because that way he couldn't be too emotional in the way that too many of the men she now knew were dependent and cloying. But he never rang and then he would often appear on her doorstop as if she was waiting for him.

After sex, Jeff always strangely remembered how his father hardly talked and his words were his actions in the way that what he collected became a museum or a huge book. He last saw him surrounded by his stuff in a Victorian country town a week or so before the funeral talking about how he was still useful because people still brought him things to fix. In fact he said the backyard was full of things he didn't have time to get to. Robin last saw her father propped up in a hospital bed in Newcastle, wizened and weak and about to die.

All those years of shift work at the steelworks – how it made him hard and so tired he couldn't or wouldn't show love to his kids. He didn't have the energy because he needed to coddle himself as everything else had been given away. Didn't have the money to buy any time, didn't have time. She had gently fondled her schoolbooks and watched as some of the other kids went on holidays to Sydney. She heard stories, of horses and of houses, which weren't mean and she tried not to feel sorry for her father when he was sentimental at Christmas and made the relatives cry. He wore overalls and his hands were never completely clean.

By December her house resembled a rubbish dump and even though he promised profusely to take things away and have a spectacular working bee one weekend, things stayed the same. Car parts and stained books lay throughout the hallway, the bedrooms and the kitchen. At first she made gentle suggestions about, how together, they could clean it up so there might be a future apart from all his history, but he ignored her even though he sounded as if he agreed. He offered to fix some things in the house, such as wonky chair legs and her ex-husband's red lawn mower. He wanted to become useful to her and have an excuse to drop over.

He made the pop up toaster work for once, but weeks turned into months and when they saw each another, their lovemaking became fitful and only isolated items disappeared from the more obvious traffic along the hall and in the kitchen.

So she decided to finish the relationship and said so one night over dinner. It was true that after sex he was more melancholy, open and relaxed, but that wasn't the time to talk because it would crack open the moment. He took it well enough (she imagined), and she knew, that he was the one who had really made it impractical the way in which he'd run away from her because he sensed that she didn't have the energy to mend both of their heavy hearts. She was the one who was visibly upset, whereas he simply left and spent more time with his mate in the house at the edge of town. Threw himself into his work and was nice to more people in case anyone got too close.

Towards the end when they told Jeff he was dying, that his heart had none of its necessary equipment in good working order, he and his mate in the house at the edge of town were restless bachelors full of bravado about loving women. They both knew that they weren't serious because that kind of talk contained truths that were often best left to literature. Jeff knew the famous quotes. Shakespearian lines that made the heart move and parts of poems that could kill you if you weren't careful. They lived like little boys in a state of dull longing. Sometimes women would visit, mostly on practical errands, and they felt feminised for a time, but Jeff was living as if he was eating his last meal.

It was nearly six months since they'd moved in together. His mate tried to keep the house free of mess and negotiate some clean places and do the washing as a way of coping. There were piles of it, because Jeff would leave his discards in the hall explaining that it was that way as it had been a long winter there wasn't any point in attending to it because it'd never dry properly. His boots were prominent next to the front door. So, feeling unco-operative, his mate only washed his own underpants.

His mate remembered the time right near the end when Jeff was set to go to his work ball and so he produced a brown suit for special occasions for washing one night. 'Take it to the dry cleaners', his mate said, 'let it stand like something special in the cleaner's racks, and when you wear it on the night you'll look like somebody.' But he would have nothing of it because, as he said, he was in too much of a rush to sort out something as trivial as that.

Weeks later, after returning from a trip north, where the winter wasn't nearly as fierce, his mate found the suit coat and pants, all alone on the clothes line out the back, flapping and fading in a fitful spring breeze. It had been raining and parts of it were wet as if it had been weeping. Jeff's personal effects had been collected up and carried away, and he imagined that the suit was moving defiantly in the wind, but there was no body to it by then. In another way, it was useful, like a scarecrow, because there was a vegetable patch in the yard, and a pile of junk, and a magpie in a huge oak tree chatting about all his treasures.

# BY THE GRACE OF GOD

'She gave Ken all of her juices – we were twins you see. She's been sucking and suckling him all his life.' It was uncharacteristic of Henry to be so direct, so unkind and circumspect, but he was upset again about why his mother didn't love him. There had been a phone call between them in his tiny house in the town. He'd been reading about the importance of social class in politics, when the call came winging up the wires from Hawthorn where she was sitting on her pink sofa next to the mahogany table in the sunroom.

It was early last summer, after all the insinuations of spring, which had promised so much and delivered little. The sunshine had been fitful, but, this day it was humid, and he came to visit me up the side path under the kitchen window with a creased brow carried along by purposeful strides. I had just finished the lawns and in doing so was hoping against hope my world might be as clean and organised as they now looked. The clippings were resting in discreet piles, and my thesis on cultural contradiction was spread out on the kitchen table in my desperate search for coherence and sense in the mess that had become my life.

Henry had been visiting for the past eight months and there were two main reasons for our meetings, philosophy and football. He heard in town that some people called me a leftie. I had taken up causes and was into conservation. But it was my Bomber beanie and his dirty red and black scarf, which initiated our first conversation outside the pie shop in the main street. 'Are you Ian?' he enquired politely. 'The rumour is that you are a Bomber supporter,' he said almost apologetically. 'I have been meaning to drop in and see you.' Then he excused himself and by way of explanation for his departure said he was in search of a book in the library about the worker's revolt of 1848.

This day though, I sat him down at the kitchen table after pushing the files to one side. I offered him baked beans but he declined them even though he looked as if he hadn't eaten for days. The day before he'd mentioned that his brother had conned him into signing away his inheritance. It had been when they lived together in the big house up on the hill overlooking the Catholic school and the railway station, during that time when they had hippy parties with skinny-dipping in the swimming pool. The dope was cheaper then, when people seemed friendlier and more prepared to experiment with one another. They at least seemed to be listening in that town away from the bright yuppie things of the city and the encroachments of jobs. People even contemplated spending the winter up north. But Ken stole his money.

'I went to Melbourne,' he said falteringly. 'I pleaded with my mother to change the papers, but she just spat like a cat and told me I was a nobody, unlike my brothers, who ran car-yards and had shares.'

Henry said he had been hit by a woman in the town; 'a great big butch bird who despises small men', as he described her. But the truth might be that she hates her dead father who'd fondled her in the bungalow in the backyard at Coburg, all those long years before she stopped men putting their thing into her. The trouble also was that Henry was caught talking politics in the health food shop and overheard in the chemist's accosting the pharmacist about the then Premier. 'And which side are you on Mr Brownlee?' he said, but poor shy Mr Brownlee could only blush and go on dispensing antibiotics to pensioners. She hit him back and front – shirt fronted him we would have said in Bomber land during one of those hectic first quarters when the teams feel each other out. He was left stretched out on the footpath on the main street of that struggling Gippsland town.

'Where did you go? What did you do?' I asked. He rose to his feet as if to avoid another blow. 'I went over to Dr Watson,' he said. 'I couldn't go to a woman because she would have just laughed,' he added. 'Are you quite sure?' I added limply, imagining that there was some image of his mother inching up into his mind and overtaking his heart. That line from Arlo Guthrie, 'there's always somebody worse off than you – but what about the last guy?' chimed inside me, for Henry had been telling me about how even the unemployed kids at Skill share laughed at him.

He took constitutionals up and down our street and along the highway leading into town where retired folks fiddled with sprinklers in the sunsets and sort of nodded at him as he went past in his funny felt hat and sunglasses. And there had been whispering – 'O there's Henry, he's a communist,' they'd say. 'Russian looking, dark and short,' someone said, so he just went back to his bungalow, to the mess and the piles of *Socialist Weeklys* on the living room floor.

'And why is it that so many people aren't ethical?' he wondered out loud. He could tell you about the Enlightenment and the power of Reason, and, as he said, the great philosophers who gave us hope of which we have so little. He loved history. We shouldn't forget what men and women do to one another,' he often said.

'You know Ian, you should get to know some foreign women, they are much more sensual than Australians,' he said. 'When I was at Melbourne University there was this marvellous Indian woman who'd read all of the Karma Sutra. She could show you a thing or two.' At that point I just had to sit down because I'd been celibate for six months and couldn't contemplate advice from someone who was only five foot four. And, after that conversation, voluptuous Asian beauties danced in my dreams on windy nights. And one night I even woke in a sweat because I thought I saw him suckling a Chinese woman in the back row of a restaurant in the city.

'Are you going to sue her?' I asked. 'The front row forward or my mother?' he asked by way of reply. 'The butch one,' I said. 'I'd like to but I'm a male and I won't get legal aid.' Then he turned to face me and he took off his cap under which there was a receding hairline and a gentle face.

'You know Ian we are now an endangered species. The feminists have infiltrated all the power structures. On one hand they want to be treated like women and on the other they dress up like business executives – and most of them are middle class.'

I couldn't face him because among some of the weirdest and most wayward and reactionary statements, there is at times a smudge of wisdom, and in his grotesque fear, I saw something that was out of control in all of us.

Last Friday night we'd watched a night football game together because he didn't have a telly and there was no heating at his place. He came around in that scarf and sat in the big armchair, bolt upright and marvelled at the young muscles on the Baby Bombers, but when one of them hit an opponent with a fist to the head, he quoted Gandhi at me.

That was last week.

He still seemed upset. There was something intent in him and he brought it up. 'You know Ian the best erotic experience I ever had was with an older man.' I blanched. 'When?' I asked. 'I was thirteen, at Silas College. He was a friend of the family, a friend of my father's,' he said unapologetically.

I recalled a conversation we'd had the week before in which he'd argued strenuously for the civil rights of paedophiles. It was in the backyard. I was checking on the fruit trees to see if they'd weathered the frost. The lemon tree looked loopy, it was sturdy enough, but the others must be pruned when the time came I concluded. The vegies were in trouble, I had not attended to them properly and the odd seasonal weather had eliminated any good luck I'd had. He'd brought up paedophilia almost by accident.

There had been a court case in town where one of the city councillors had to leave for molesting a young boy, and across from the courthouse, a group of women demonstrated in the carpark with placards suggesting that he was a danger to all women everywhere. Henry had called in and over the remains of lunch delivered a long monologue about how these people were demanding their rights and neglecting those of others. But that day I couldn't pinpoint his prose, because he was usually so theoretical and his search for the perfect social system, which might eliminate demons, had been a support, even when he had been in hospital after the bashing. He was learning Maths at TAFE, where its clean, unremitting logic seemed like a skeleton into which other flawed and contradictory souls shouldn't venture. He said his teacher was always searching for the perfect shape away from human mess. He told me that Leon Trotsky wrote great prose and that he had, in fact, inspired him into forming an unemployed workers group in the town. But nothing happened.

There were other conversations over which I shuddered, now that I recall. He babysat children for some of the single mothers in town. He thought it was because they didn't see him as a threat and they didn't pay him, but I let it pass in those dangerous days.

'Who was this man?' I asked gingerly. He wouldn't identify him by any name, but instead insisted that he'd been a caring person who had wished him no harm, and as far as he knew he had done him none. I had though become very angry that day in the garden about paedophilic rights. 'There are taboos Henry and that is one. You were below the age of consent,' I shouted back at his protestations that I was a puritan who was bourgeois in my beliefs. 'It was the highlight of my life,' he stressed, rising to rinse out his coffee cup and take off his footy scarf.

I couldn't bring myself to ask whether his horrid brothers and his fearful mother knew about it in their pretentious Hawthorn house. His father was later to die an awful death and Henry insisted on nursing him through the worst. He wanted to take away their pain but he couldn't understand how deeply they despised him for trying.

He nearly became a teacher once but the student round in the country high school didn't work out, a colleague told me. Henry suggested to the headmaster that students should know about under-age sex. 'It's all political,' he told the headmaster.

We never discussed it again, yet, at the edges of philosophy and football, he sometimes interjected reflections on how wonderful it would be to be taken under the wing of a great coach or an inspiring teacher. They were dangerous days, for the big answers were all gone and it was uncool to even talk of the brotherhood of men and women. Madonna was mocking him. And, at the end of that month someone broke into his place and stole the few valuables that were left.

# TWO DOGS

She always talked about her dog, it was like her, she said, a gritty female who'd survived on the streets. That dog had defended her puppies from attacks from marauding males in back lanes in the city, so one shouldn't get too close, because Sally might snap, out of fear, even if she liked you, and one could never be quite sure whether it was a warning, or a come on. Jenny cared for the creature, and in the time I knew her, she walked it almost every day along a nearby beach. It reminded me of my own dog from years before, a willowy German shepherd with an aquiline head and long tail – the kind of creature that'd smile in ways that only dogs can. The kind of creature that inspires loyalty even as it strains against your weight and refuses to bow to anything other than itself.

She let me walk her dog once – we'd been talking about relationships, which of course should have been warning enough to anyone capable of reading signs, for there are always indications in the things animals do and in which humans prefer not to see. Around a local park, a couple of streets from where she lived, and then across the football oval, Sally straining at her leash, insisting on interrogating smells and signals. My dog used to do that when we went off into the bush behind the house and along dilapidated fence lines that marked our imaginary territories – there were dangerous unmarked mine shafts that dropped in front of you, fox scats surrounding incongruous rock formations, and a loneliness that only words could ever scurry after. Sally was similar; the kind of dog one can't help but look at in almost aristocratic ways which people who have everything feel they need to relate to. A pretty dog, a cuddly dog, like the one I'd once had, whom I always think of during busy times and when there is no reason to do so. I wanted Sally to be my friend, and, there was a chance, as I'm good with animals, because they sense I won't hurt them. Maybe I have the right kind of smell. Jenny seemed to think so because she initiated intimacy. She called in for coffee and suggested we go out on a date, and after that, 'come back to my place,' which I did, and we started getting close.

The trouble was I think I got too familiar for her frame. Jenny didn't say it as such, but there had been signs and slightly elongated phrases suggesting I shouldn't care so much, because what would happen could become something we couldn't cope with.

Sally reminded me of my old dog, how he was like the child one would yearn for, during those first winters on the land with the frightening shafts and whistling secrets that couldn't be spoken. How much I loved him – 'every hair on his head' to a questioner once – 'every hair on his head' to the friend from Latin America who'd come from a country where rich people treat animals better than people. The beautiful tail – I'm looking at it now, I can almost touch it, his tongue, the fur on his back, the erect ears, the unjudging eyes, and his delicate posturing.

Walking around the oval that day was the first time I'd let another animal get so close. I'd never wanted to taint my memories of the best dog in the world, the kindest friend a man could ever have, and of when he clawed moaning at the small mound we'd made for the kind of ceremony you construct to control grief. It was between a clump of trees on a rise overlooking the valley, a few friends and a list of imaginary ones looking on, late enough in the afternoon for the sweep of lorikeets to come on cue up from the south. A slight wind, an almost disdainful kangaroo gazing at us as if we were the horizon rather than the middle distance, and the new dog unable to grasp what had gone on. I loved him, but he died, like some old dogs do, after a stroke to his left side.

'He's not your dog, you know', Jenny said, as we came around an intersection after looking at a rambling house in an indiscriminate suburban street. I took it in, as you do, because the conversation had been expansive and somewhat problematic, about having more children in the rambling house, how she was happiest when that happened, even though the father of her first wasn't anywhere around. 'The happy hormones kick in and I forget all that silly writing stuff and the problems of the world,' she had insisted.

Sally had been gazing up into my eyes like only attractive dogs can do, with a look across her mouth suggesting that I too could be a friend. Another unjudgemental creature I thought. My dog Boof was dead, but he wasn't you know, I grasped at that in case he was whisked away again. 'He is not your dog you know', she was quite adamant, in case I got too close, almost as if some of her love might end up being halved, or deep down become blocked.

I'd been seeing a lot of her, in that house next to the railway line where freight trains rumbled in an arc past the back fence and then up past my way. 'You could leave a note on the train and have it delivered the same day', she once quipped, which was so sweet, so old fashioned and nerdy for someone so assertively *with it*. A time when spinning stories connected, reassembled and ran away.

My memory has been fading, or fragmenting slightly, because, I'm not sure now that it was outside the rambling house that Jenny said that Sally was hers. It could have been on the beach when I kissed her and there was something about 'be careful, Sally doesn't know you, she might get jealous', which was incongruous because the dog was being relatively trivial, just like mine, as it skipped among seaweed and ran at angles. The week before, she had given me a photo frame for Boof shocked it seemed that I'd only had him as a loose photo in the top drawer at work, and only looked at him for the first time in years because I briefly got the courage from her. He remained face down for months after that because I couldn't face even the beautiful things he had brought to me and what I'd left behind in the place I couldn't face.

There was always a test of some sort, along the lines of, 'I test out my partners on how they relate to my son', a cautionary story of boyfriends who only lasted three months at the max, either because they couldn't relate to kids or to the dog, told in a dead pan delivery during a Johnny Depp movie where the main character ate his victims and served them up as meaty delicacies. Life, it seemed, was the kind of thing that happens when everyone is coming and going.

Back to the dogs – Sally was talking a lot and my new friend was joyfully bounding about, being silly. I of course, was very silly because I was sick of being serious, the yearning feeling was all but gone, and even the funeral and all the other small deaths were morphing into something else at last. I was being very silly – as I never thought I wouldn't be caught in the moment where grief regrouped and came knocking. But while I was being silly my memory caught stray lines of dialogue. Yes – outside the rambling house, on the day when we walked around the streets of her suburb, she said, 'do you want kids? You know I can see myself in that house, there's this great big backyard for them to play, hordes of them, and the front yard is big enough for parties on the lawn.'

I'd lost control as it didn't seem to matter all that much, because the next thing might be an interesting place to visit, something exciting to sniff out, or a place where there was always sun, so I didn't take it in, in case it caught me out. There was another conversation I recall. Something about being too old to grow up with (or was it too young?), which, now I think about it, wasn't all about me. Sally was straining at her leash as we walked across the park to where the railway track separated the suburb from itself and I imagined that maybe I didn't have the right smell.

Months later, I told Jenny by email that I was writing a book told from the perspective of a dog, where the narrator was down on the ground, sniffing out stuff, that kind of thing, and she replied with confidence, because she was pregnant again, 'cool, that's really cool' came the inflection.

# MISSING OUT ON INDY

When you miss out on most things in life pretty well everything other than the everyday becomes attractive. Melanie worked in one of those jobs where you have to smile a lot and be nice to people you normally wouldn't have home for dinner. But because it was in the service industry she had to be pleasant to anyone with money. She was a receptionist and booking person in a resort a block from the beach, a place that was by the time she came to work for them, slightly faded. Its early '80s architecture wasn't four star because all the new buildings had jacuzzis, swish angles and a different idea of light. They were the kind of buildings that announced themselves in no uncertain terms, and the people who rented for a week or two caught a glimpse of how stylish some people's lives can become.

Melanie's place suffered from stiff competition but it held its own because it was good value for people with kids, and she looked up to Adrian who owned the management rights. He was aspirational, gruff in a sensitive sense, and matey to the blokes who came to stay. In his merry moments he imagined that the place could be like a low rise Marriot with a renovation and a change of clientele. His staff dressed well, in tasteful uniforms that weren't made in China, and when they showed people around the complex, they exhibited an understated style.

Adrian was like many of his male guests. He was once a tradesman in a regional centre with a four-wheel drive and dreams of serious money. He loved his four-wheel drive because you could sit up higher than the people in sedans and station wagons and believe that, in one way at least, it separated him out from the rest. He realised that there was more to her, but he was the boss so she shut up and tried hard to look immaculate every morning when she had to answer the phone and listen to his plans.

Living on the coast, Melanie couldn't help but meet people. At work, contacts were fragmented, fleeting, and never stable, because the place was always changing. But on Friday or Saturday nights she usually went to the local drinking holes and nightclubs with one or two of her girlfriends. Single girls who loved 'Sex in the City', and could remember most of the stock scenarios and discuss at length how the situations related to their knowledge of men. They were also much the same age, late thirties and early forties; one had been married before, but Melanie never. But on the coast there was always another stream of gorgeous girls so it was a question of finding bars that weren't used by the kids.

One night they went to Stables, a place up in the entertainment district with only enough light to delineate gender and the difference between drinks. It was so loud you couldn't hear what anyone was saying, which was just as well because it staved off the disappointment of finding out what someone might really be like. In any case, to dwell on such things would be to miss the point of such excursions.

Indy had come to town, a streetcar race attracting streams of petrol heads and drivers with Brazilian and Italian surnames. That night at Stables, they met Rod, Lee and Charlie all of whom said they owned tyre dealerships in Tasmania, and Indy, they said, was a tax trip, where they could gauge the grip of the popular brands under extreme circumstances. Lee said, 'stuff the tyres I've come for the local talent.'

Whether it was the fitful light, or the overpowering music, no one was quite sure, but Melanie ended up chatting to Rod who was of medium build with brown shortish hair and a body which suggested that he worked out in his spare time. It wasn't possible to determine whether he was married, or in a relationship (but he didn't have a ring), and she took a shine to him in the way that talking to strangers in bars can be entertaining. They were similar ages and there wasn't any obvious educational difference that might encourage insecurity later on. She'd long decided that since she'd left school in year ten, there wasn't much point looking for a man who might want to discuss difficult subjects. In any case that's what her girlfriends were for. And, there are times in all our lives when communication and closeness is just a mess of work.

Politics didn't figure in her life, well not that thing to do with politicians and the smell of power, except for when her boss made comments about how the Prime Minister was doing a good job keeping out unwanted Arab refugees. 'Never repeat that in front of Dubai businessmen they are big property investors on the coast', the boss said. 'Because we all need to know which side our bread is buttered on in a tourist place', he added. He tried to look down on them as if they were refugees, but he couldn't afford to. And she agreed, not just out of loyalty, but because her father was a refugee from Europe after the war and he desperately wanted to fit in. She wanted to be a good girl, the way her boss always wanted her to be efficient every morning after she'd struggled with her make-up on the way to work. She detested refugees because no one made a fuss of her. 'Let em drown', she once said to some married friends who were talking about the issue.

Drinking though is differently risky, and easier, and you don't have to be a good girl for once, and anyway it's better than talking in daylight to unhappily married balding men who have no money. At least the boys from Launceston might have some.

Rod gave her the number of his mobile – scribbled it out on the back of a beer coaster, in the half light under a kind of red lamp next to a young girl's leg that he'd been fooling around with. But Melanie didn't appear to notice. She was sad like that, seemingly oblivious to moments of humiliation because to show offence might have meant that she'd never have a chance. When she and her friends went on the town feminism was a distant, awkward dream, the sort of thing educated women in big cities carried on about who didn't seem to have to negotiate the kind of greedy need the boys from Launceston recognised. As she sometimes said to her girlfriends, 'I don't have an education, and no one is going to leave me any money.'

She'd spent ten years in Japan where a half-decent looking foreign woman is made to feel special. She followed her Australian boyfriend, but that palled because he didn't like the crowds and closed spaces. So she stayed and became a hostess in Tokyo's entertainment district and became special to salary men and seedy characters dressed in black, which was better than hospitality on the coast with its penchant for teenagers with blonde hair and pretty smiles. There was so much going on in Japan she could work every night and never really be caught having to sit at home, be herself, see her unmade face and watch her spirits sag. She became Sumio's girlfriend, but she came back to Australia because she didn't want to play second fiddle to his wife. It was back to the coast, but by then girlfriends were married with a few kids and couldn't talk for hours and go out drinking.

She rang up Rod a few days after the first meeting in the nightclub. The boys had been having a great time in the days leading up to the car race. He said something about inviting her to the Indy party they'd be having at the Casablanca – an apartment block crowned in Spanish mission phallic style turrets.

'You should come, just ring me on my mobile from the foyer two hours before the race – we'll come down and get you', he added in a tone slightly like a salesman. She had met many guys like him, the way everything was slightly unfinished and promising. She'd always had this thing against men she called 'blokey', which was shorthand for the guys she grew up with. Her girlfriends kind of agreed when they got into their slightly pissed sex in the city moods with lines like – 'you know he's a really nice guy but he is too blokey', the implication being that somewhere there was someone who was sophisticated who'd make the everyday go away.

The morning of the Indy party, she spent a lot of it on the phone to her friend Julie trying to glean advice about what she should wear, whether the black strapless dress was too daring or bloody obvious, that kind of thing. But, by lunchtime she was ready and arranged to meet her married friends a few blocks from the Casablanca, an apartment building facing the racetrack in the heart of Surfers Paradise. They met in the lobby in garments they imagined might be appropriate for celebrating Indy. Sue was tastefully attired with a strong suggestion of cleavage in the skimpy black dress.

At the nominated time she rang his number, but the mobile rang and rang, in fact rang out so that the message bank recording came on. She'd tried the number he gave her for nearly an hour. The lobby of the apartments was cool but she was sweating as she waited just in case anyone answered.

She was with the married couple. They were nice enough people who saw their weekends as a time for entertainment rather than desperate searching. They seemed secure and tried to calm her down even though she said she didn't need it because she wasn't distressed, so they took her to Matildas on the corner of the highway and Omero St., a renovated pub that accommodates packs of pissed kids every Friday night. She didn't want to keep ringing the mobile number again and again, so she felt stupid, because the married couple were calm and reassuring and concerned about how she felt. They'd been to enough parties to last a lifetime, but she was distraught and maniacally shifted about in her seat in between visits to the toilet. She tried not to cry but the pub was a crazy place full of shouting people and dorky boys wearing reversed baseball caps.

Indy had started, there was a great roar from the next block, and from where they were sitting they could see the southern end of the track behind a row of plastic barriers. It was an invasive roar unlike the sound of the sea. A roar that screamed rather than reassured, a sound made for people who felt out of control and slightly small. There were thousands of sightseers – clusters of skimpily clad teenage girls and young men in tee-shirts, petrol heads from places like Warwick and Mackay where social hierarchies are either more rigid or more visible than on the Coast. She remembered her mum saying to her once that when young men race around town in loud cars they are saying, 'Look at me, I'm here, I'm alive, don't forget me.' Here on the coast, instead of in some inland town, their screams were drowning out in alcohol and the professional drivers were taking away all the attention.

The steady supply of cocktails had made her teary and she often broke off the conversation to call the mobile number. Yet again there was no answer. Maybe he was too busy with the catering she imagined, but it was one of those stories we make up for ourselves to make humiliation bearable, of trying to reason out surreal facts and feral events. Her speech was slightly slurred. She told the married couple stories of the time ten years ago, when she would never have waited in the lobby of any building for any length of time. She told them stories about parties on cruise boats on the seaway, and of cocktails with a better class of person than just another blokey tyre-dealer from Tasmania.

They told her that she didn't need to go to the party, it wouldn't have been any good anyway, and tried to be reassuring as much as people with a sense of security can. After several hours they drove her home and when they dropped her off at her place they told her not to worry.

She didn't get in touch with the married couple for about a month. All of the tyre dealers and try – hards had gone back to where they came from – suburban estates with curving cul-de-sacs and self contained courts with traffic humps, where it is impossible to get up any self respecting speed in the hotrod. Places made for convenience rather than adventure, but from where it was sometimes possible to see the sea or some land that wasn't totally tamed.

She had been out on the town with the girls a couple of times she said. It was better than staying home. Work was a grind. If she met anyone interesting there was never any time to have a conversation and then it might seem unprofessional. She never heard from Rod, but she left him a text message saying he was a bastard.

They had been to Stables, but this time it was a different crowd she said, 'less blokey and a bit quieter'. It had been possible to talk and they played one of their sex in the city games, pick the gay. Who's got a hairy chest then? She looked thinner, but she was her usual chatty self except for when the married couple got serious about politics and then she went distant. 'It was a fun night', she said. Mark from Dreamworld was there talking about a job that there might be for her working with tour parties. He had a mate called Wayne who said he was flying helicopters in Bali, trips out of Nusa Dua and the other resorts for tourists.

He'd been in the Whitsunday's, he said, Hamilton, and Airlie Beach, the kind of places, which try to make out that people who live in suburbs or towns are refugees from pleasure, inhabitants of another world. He'd be going back to Bali in a couple of days, she said. She liked him, he wasn't really blokey because he'd travelled a lot, and there was something about his voice, but this time though she didn't get the mobile number. She could have got it from Mark but let it slide in case he mightn't answer or remember her.

Work ground on as usual. The occasional strangely unattached male from some suburb in Sydney or Melbourne asked her out after meeting her at the resort, but she never went with them. The girls as per usual took her to Stables but she felt a bit ridiculous because the place was packed with blonde Swedish girls with toned figures and angelic smiles. She'd look for Wayne but he never came. Mark said that he had gone to Bali to work at the Sheraton in Nusa Dua, hadn't heard anything from him but was sure he was having a great time. 'He usually does overseas', he said.

So she decided to go without contacting him or delving into the details of how she'd get to where he was. It'd be a bit like signing up for one of those Internet introduction agencies. She had a vague memory of his face and there was a chance that he wouldn't work out but she was quite used to that.

* * *

Flying to Bali brought back nearly two decades of travelling to exotic destinations, of noticing how places change when people insist upon enjoying themselves in the shortest possible time. The Garuda flight was full of the type of people she imagined were usually the clients of the resort she worked in and where she was going to, married couples with a couple of teenage kids. The wives (as she knew all too well) were worth watching, the way they tried to be condescending when talking to the airhostesses, trivial complaints about the refresher towels and comments about how their husbands shouldn't be disturbed because they'd been busy all week in they're businesses.

Those women thought how they could have been airhostesses but hadn't, because in Rockhampton you have a couple of kids before you are thirty, otherwise people think you could be infertile or flighty. They thought about where they'd parked the Range Rover in the long-term carpark, and how insignificant it seemed from up in the air surrounded by hundreds of other Range Rovers. What was the point in buying the bloody thing in the first place when the long-term carpark had hundreds of them, but it would be different when they got home?

The plane touched down at Denpasar and the customs officials were polite. Outside in the heat, the obligatory holding up of holiday pickups reminded her of Coolangatta airport but that was mannered, ordered, this was grotty and urgent to her experienced tourist operator's eye. She decided to stay one night in Kuta, up near Legian beach, to make her plans, in a place she knew that had bungalows away from the street surrounding a swimming pool. Wayne was about fifty kilometres away. The next morning she took a taxi to the Sheraton Nusa Dua and she found him working behind the main desk. Outside, a helicopter rose from the front lawn with a presidential flourish.

She asked him why he was working on reception. 'What about

the helicopter'? He had the grace to look sheepish for a minute. 'He was working up to that,' he said. All he needed was a promotion. 'Four months, tops!' But he asked her if she wanted a drink with a kind of crooked smile that implied she was a mate and was in on his secret.

Over the next few days he worked but always had time to see her at six when he had finished checking in families from Engadine, Frankston and Castle Hill. He bought her sunset coloured cocktails and one night broke a yellow hibiscus from the bush and tucked it behind her ear.

She liked him, even if he was only an admissions clerk as she was. Wayne was faithful, considerate and independent like a type of native dog. Simple in the way he spoke with bullshitty flourishes such as the stuff about being a helicopter pilot. He simply wouldn't have understood how anyone wouldn't have been able to see through the blarney. After all, Australian guys like him sometimes send up pretension, especially back home on the coast where some people put on a lot of face.

She could see how things might become more solid. She could see that she might stay there for a while. She began to see that she could like herself. But as a month went by she disliked feeling comfortable and she was always sadder, powerful yet more powerless than he could ever be. So, on the flight back to Brisbane (sitting next to no one), she wondered whether her girlfriends were going to Stables next Saturday and she knew that it wasn't really worth the effort.

# GOOD COFFEE (CIRCA 2002)

Helen loved good coffee and living in inner Melbourne. She often found it in the trendy cafes, particularly on Saturday mornings where she'd flick at the papers over breakfast with friends – a menagerie of eggs, bacon, and some black clothing and the colour supplement of *The Good Weekend*.

But she had a friend Wendy who lived up north on the Gold Coast in Queensland, an old friend, in fact a kind of dear friend with whom she could share some secrets. Their stories always became meandering monologues, and because they'd known each other for so long, common characters from childhood, and references from a closer past linked them.

Wendy went up, about five years before, had left one of those dark Melbourne winters for a place where most people behaved it seemed as if they were on holiday. That of course, was a relief, because even men who worked in banks wore shorts, and most of the women wore very little, which was great if you weren't into fashion. Wendy had gone north, and liked to stick it up her southern friends as their winter approached by inviting them up to stay, with promises of warmer days and ways of letting off steam. But the truth was also that many of the conversations she had up north seemed more outward than inward, and that was a difference, even social commentators could remark upon. There are roots and connections even if they remain in shallow ground and are planted in more turbulent times.

So Wendy asked Helen up to stay and it was organized over the internet on a budget airline almost in the speed of sound – she'd pick her up at Coolangatta airport on Wednesday night at 7 pm, she said in one of the messages, 'remember to bring your bathers,' she added, 'and some sun screen', which was a slight assault to Helen's southern sensibilities, to remind her that warmth and comfort could be somewhere else.

So Helen planned her trip to the last detail, almost like as if she was going overseas, and added in another message, 'do they have any good coffee up there?' She had of course been schooled into believing that Queensland was that land of Joh, an inarticulate Premier who rooted for farmers, a kind of capitalist in the good times and bastardised socialist in the bad. He reminded her of some of her unspeakable male relatives, of her father, who had often been intolerant and bossy when she had been a girl. Queensland was also a place of indifferent heat and big distances that made one feel small if you went out in it too often, and even though the Gold Coast had a wall of skyscrapers along the beach front, 'in no way could it be a *city*', she often said to people. But she liked her old friend, and, although her choice of residence was rather strange, there was no doubt that getting out of Melbourne was a good thing in winter. They could chat and look at men and other women.

Wendy's apartment looked out over the sea, the emphasis all around being outward, across the ocean, out to the mountains in the distance; people were in fact specks, rarely ever in focus. But if you looked closely enough they might be on the back of a wave, or hailing a cab, or sunbaking on a balcony below, and the good thing was that there were anonymous stories that you could make up for these figures without the hindrance of any set history or too many allegiances.

She liked entertaining and when Helen came on the Wednesday night she made dinner and it stood proudly on the table. She had also planned out the week, as she liked doing, because she wanted to show Helen that Queensland wasn't quite as backward as Melbournians imagined. 'It has culture tucked away beyond the surface', she said in one email. 'Six community theatres in the hinterland, a kind of pressure behind where the waves wash in', she said. 'Well go the races. You should see the horrible fashions', she added, in a gesture towards southern reconciliation. Maybe there we can get some good coffee, she thought; the question grated as there wasn't really anywhere close by as people mainly drank beer. But it was true there were a few places now that all those southerners had moved in. On her first night, Helen slept well, and in the morning a troupe of talkative parakeets danced and chortled on the balcony railing in case she had forgotten where she was.

The itinerary for the first morning was surfing down near Coolangatta, a great place, as there were still cream brick sixties holiday flats and the odd elongated Queenslander in a back street behind the shops. The surf club had been renovated but it was still somewhere where ordinary families could go and have a smorgasbord for seven bucks and the beach was still free.

Secretly, Wendy thought that 'Cooly' might be a good place for 'good' coffee, but she was unsure as she'd forgotten some of the brands and the cute names in her time on the coast. She brought her husband Ron along because he liked 'Cooly' (as they called it), something about it being one of the last places where working class people went for their holidays. He was old fashioned like that as somehow he just couldn't get with *it* – whatever *it* was.

He wanted to go to the beach for the remarkable light and the way the sea played with the sand – simple kinds of pleasures, as he too was a refugee from Melbourne winters and what he gruffly called 'lifestyle' affectations. Life there had been disappointing, long lulls of desperation sprinkled with flashes of insight, and he thought of himself as unpretentious, but Wendy dismissively called it 'another one of your egalitarian conceits'.

So they got to 'Cooly', the sun was luminous as usual, so bright, even in winter you needed sunglasses to park properly because the reflections were dangerous in tight spaces. They had all brought their bathers but Helen was gruff about swimming, worried about who'd see her exposed legs and she'd get sand in her clothes, 'there was just too much sand at the beach', she said, 'and it could spread out when they got back in the car', so they decided to start off with a coffee. There were a few bistro type places in the street behind the Esplanade facing south, and the light wasn't as bright, and Ron really hoped that they'd have skinny lattes, long blacks and other exotically named concoctions, so that she'd relax a bit, 'chill out', have a smile and stop talking about her problems with boyfriends.

You see there were times when he felt like Jeremiah, especially when after talking to her his head became a screen of rolling clichés: 'get over it', 'life's not like that', 'nothings perfect', 'open yourself out to new experiences' etc, etc.' The cafe though (according to Helen) wasn't up to scratch, 'it doesn't look right, look they are only serving cappuccinos', she remarked at that place where the footpath meets the doorway, and it wasn't the time to debate the relative merits of coffees when so many people were only intent on consumption.

No one wanted a fuss, least of all the waitress who had just learned that they'd run out of soymilk. The place next door wasn't much chop either Helen announced in different tones. 'But that's all there is', Ron insisted, but she persisted. 'There must be somewhere that isn't blokey, has some arty posters on the wall and where people aren't loud.' No luck, well not by that stage of the day.

Helen insisted on looking at a map of the Coast just in case it pointed out places of culinary significance, and for a second she had a fantasy that there would be coffee signs as well as bus stops and markings that showed post offices and the like, but there was nothing except for a strip of settlement that said 'Palm Beach' stretching northward across the Melways. 'What's there', she asked. 'Nothing much – a boringly beautiful strip of sand with new apartments and a highway.' 'Are there shops?' 'Yes, but I doubt there is any good coffee, take my word for it,' Ron insisted. But they got back in the car, cruised past the bird sanctuary at Currumbin where happiness can always be heard, the bridge over the creek, and came to what the locals call 'Palmy'. Ron knew that it'd be a waste of time because the first response from a local to Helen's question – 'do you have any good coffee', was only 'you should try Safeway love, I know they have got Nescafe', a man said with a wry grin. They searched but came up with nothing of choice other than a stainless steel machine at 7-Eleven that coughed out brown slimy coagulated granules.

'Palmy' wasn't any good, but Helen suggested they go back to Currumbin where they found a beaut place, 'Steve's beach café' which had passable lattés, but she couldn't help talking about Michael who she been going out with for a couple of months, an IT professional, a really nice guy, but he wasn't much into art and by the time he finished work he'd drank enough coffee for the day. She wanted a pick up, he it seemed, wanted to calm down when night came.

Ron was getting stroppy, as it was one thing to be polite about shepherding friends around the landscape, and quite another having that disrespected by people who only saw anything different through their eyes. 'A lack of respect', he could hear his head saying. They had a focaccia, which she said wasn't hot enough, but the waitress explained that it wasn't as necessary in Queensland as down south, which was hardly satisfying, to say the least.

It had been two years or so since Helen had been up, and it was remarkable how her story hadn't changed and indeed how much hadn't changed about all the bigger stories on the TV of catastrophe and drama. The link could have been there, but few people ever talked about it in case the private became too public. But Helen talked as if nothing could change privately, the private seemed to be curling up and dying, like real talk. She was gesturing out across the coast and it seemed as if the sea was throwing her back like the tide. Wendy was also irritated, because, although she liked good coffee, it really wasn't all that important in the scheme of things. She wanted Helen to be a friend for she had things to confess, good coffee might be the lubricant, but trying so hard for what would break the ice, only destroyed everything. Was it Ron's fault for being stroppy or Helen's for being fussy? Somewhere in the distance between, there was of course a place where no one cared.

After Currumbin, there were a string of suburbs that had once been beach holiday places in another time for other generations. Helen was still rather manic about the particularity of her desires and good coffee was the call. Immediately north, the headland at Burleigh Heads rose like a beacon for the search and for the pleasure boats out in the current. The word Burleigh is a great sound in itself, and it, like Cooly, had been a great place for families from the suburbs for over thirty years. There is a park next to the bowling club for the oldies, and even now, a few shops that sell handicrafts woven in old fashion ways. But good coffee, Ron remembered, is all the go, and even he, was feeling confident about the chance of satisfying Helen's desire.

Opposite the park, he remembered a good coffee shop, where he'd been once with his brother-in-law, when he had been up on a visit. Graeme had particularly liked the cappuccino in a mug because there was your money's worth, because Graeme, he remembered, was once heard to say that small servings on big white plates left too much to the imagination. That though was years ago, and even with such doubts creeping in, surely the place had something for her, some Italian thing or other that would let her imagine she was having a more interesting life with more romantic people. But the latte was a flop and it must be said – wasn't hot enough, meaning that Helen performed and made the waitress feel small because she felt bad. They were jangled, getting in and out of the car for good coffee meant that the day was only stops and starts rather than a smooth story.

There were a few places left, as Helen explained brandishing the *Melways* across the front seat. 'What is this Miami place?' she intoned. 'An American imitation?' she asked Ron. 'I thought you liked Americans?' he retorted. 'I like intelligent Americans, but quite honestly, their architecture is appalling', she replied. 'On the whole they are an example of how crass some people can become when they have too much money. Australia's going the same way, except for perhaps in Melbourne which resists the influence, or tries too.' It was a bold statement for someone so fussy, Ron thought, but by that stage he was past nuance and into the sweep of things. Miami then was no good as it only had another renovated surf club and a couple of fish shops struggling next to a giant servo, perhaps in the way they have things in parts of America.

Somehow, at the sight of the towers of Broadbeach the topic of Wayne came up, by which time Wendy had about had enough, for even she seemed to be fading and wanted to lie down across the back seat of the car and have a cry. Wayne worked as a pilot in rural Victoria, Helen had it seemed liked the pilot idea, but the closest thing to a good coffee shop to where he worked was the main pie shop in Benalla. He went there for the vanilla slices and he hardly came down to Melbourne, and sometimes there were grease stains on his fingers, which reminded her of a time when most men worked with their hands. 'I liked him, but we didn't do much together or have much in common apart from the sex. It was awkward going places with him because he couldn't talk about intelligent things.'

Across from where they parked the car two giant white pelicans sat on a railing outside McDonalds because the rumour was that the staff had been getting rid of old fish stock. They were bulbous, nodding and chomping on the food in their beaks. Great big things that didn't give stuff about what anyone thought and who should have been back in the wild.

The coffee searchers found Sergio's, which had an entrance down from the Holiday Inn, next to a nice-looking bottle shop decked out in blue shades and some black. Broadbeach had solved the problem of hoons in fast cars by building traffic humps and ridiculous roundabouts and there were very smart cars parked out the front, and Ron noticed the toned figure of the captain of the Brisbane Lions with his bleached girlfriend walking across the road, but sensibly kept it to himself as it might reduce the general picture. Feral facts for shifting times, he concluded, noting how his head was hurting from holding in half clichés.

Leaving out the piercing light and squinting, it was possible to imagine there that there was a cosmopolitan strip of some significance on the Coast, after all their walking and driving. Further north, it would become positively multicultural, that's if you wanted it in your face, but here, Helen seemed content with a very nice latte and the sight of her profile on a mirrored wall. She really could have been anywhere, for that matter. The others sipped at their coffee, and swallowed their tears.

# SNIPPING

Johnny couldn't quite remember how long it had been since he started worrying about his country. At first, he thought, it had been in scrappy ways, say at work when any ideals he had were reduced to mindless paperwork that sapped the brain and fenced in the imagination, but it became broader, so he took to taking long car trips which proved to be briefly liberating, taking off on the first hint of a weekend when his mind seemed less crowded.

The countryside around his city was close; quick to get to as there was no traffic to speak of, and before long openness overcame constriction. In summer, there were beige fields that made up a quivering horizon, becoming mirages if the light was at a certain angle. He was determined to find what he imagined were the 'third' spaces of his country, the idea of the gap between what had been developed and wildness.

He made many such trips, but often all he saw was decaying city industry and agricultural production. One weekend in an exercise in aimlessness he took the car past the large river into Mallee country where there was a long string of dead towns on a highway between places. The man at the general store said that people came there to hide in the bush, and then to die. He said it, just like that – there was no reflection to speak of, his speech like the light was sharp at the edges, and squeezed dry of generosity, and it was then that Johnny felt that the little place was where he could escape to, as the city, he thought, was always clogged by status and acts of performance.

Yes, Johnny had been worrying about where his country was going which was pretty silly as he should have only been concerned about where he was heading, instead of being aimless like many people. Some friends on Face book posted almost every day about environmental destruction and the bestiality of politicians in righteous language. He had read again *The Lucky Country* by Donald Horne who had wondered about whether his country would outlast its luck, and it had been a year of terrorism talk and another battle for its soul.

He too was becoming intolerant and unable to listen to chatter, so it wasn't long before he knew that he'd go to live in the little town with only a handful of houses, one shop and a fire brigade shed. According to his few friends, Johnny was a 'type' of puritan attracted to the overall dryness of his country with particular quirks such as when he was once quoted as saying after a few drinks, 'I am suspicious of people who do sexy things in water, in the shower you get clean but having sex is about getting dirty.'

The town had to be far enough away so that he wouldn't be seduced back into work, where he might imagine that he was important, and could change things, have stimulating discussions which seemed to go in circles, and consolidate like-minded friends.

The town straddled the highway. Everything about it shouted decline, the faded Goodyear tyre sign on the deserted garage, the outdated brand of ice-creams on the derelict supermarket, dying deciduous attempts at gardens in the remaining houses, and the amateurish graffiti on the wheat silos next to the railway line.

Over the horizon there were stories of people who grew marijuana beyond fence lines and of a few refugee families from Syria who were working on one of the grazing properties. They were sometimes seen in the shop.

The man in the shop said that it was good that a new person could make the place their home, but his enthusiasm was unenthusiastic, yet he explained that there was a house vacant, next to, 'the one with the old hippy artwork in the front yard', he added. 'You would have seen it, a mosaic – the reds, oranges and blues stand out against the stubborn gum trees. You can hear a wind chime.'

Johnny really didn't have much to leave behind so it wasn't a wrench going to a place where there was little to look at. If you excluded all the straggly eucalyptus trees and the stunted Mallee scrub, there was next to nothing for the European eye; perhaps a carpet of resistance from one angle, and a formless pattern of survival from another. What would he do with himself? He could write about his country, he'd been worrying about it, and even on those longish car trips, he had been making notes from what people talked about in the petrol stations and truck stops he came across. That didn't seem to make sense when he got back to the city as the pace closed back on him, and he knew then that he really didn't have the heart. He was anxious that the angle might be wrong, and whose angle was it anyway, and to write from a country town might be a cliché? Too many courses in literary theory, he mused. He was also a coward, perpetually wondering whether writing books could change anything.

There was road kill on the highway, always crows cleaning up the carcasses, and then flying off as his car approached, the odd dingo disappearing into the scrub. There were so few people anywhere near the place so he imagined he saw someone he knew sitting up in on-coming cars, but the speed prevented identification, and outside, when he stopped on occasions, a silence that seeped. The man in the shop though was more forthcoming in his clipped way. 'On really hot days you know, the gum trees murmur and titter; they are threatening, especially when there is no wind. Some have been here for over a hundred years', he added. 'They see it all, yet it could be the dead blacks having a go. That is why the trees love bush fires, because they want to clean us out.'

Johnny's idea was that, for a time at least, the place might give him enough of an angle to what he was worried about with his country. Even if he didn't write it down, it might be there, so he had to organize the move, pretty soon, take with him what mattered, and try not to be so worried. He just wanted people to shut up as he had become known on social media for rants about individualism taking over everything and that selfishness was now the norm.

The move to the town wasn't all that traumatic as he didn't have much to move. His flat in the city only had essentials and his books were in store in one of the suburbs. All in all it only took a week of changing contact details, resign from his job as an archivist at the State Library where he always had to record details and different moments, and organize a removal van. He gave the driver very precise delivery details as there was so little to find he could easily miss it when he got there.

The rundown house was similar to any of the houses, in any of the towns, along that road. When he finally drove in, he had slowed to a speed that would have once been appropriate for a school crossing so he saw again the remains of the 'hippy' house, of which the man at the shop had also mumbled about it being an 'unsuccessful collective' around about the time when John Lennon was shot and the sixties and early seventies finally died. 'But it was also lack of water and the summer heat sent some of them mad – a couple of them were seen staggering along the highway picking up thrown away food and drink containers.'

Johnny's new house was a weatherboard with a large garden front and back with many gums and a sprinkling of half dead fruit trees. The gums dropped their bark in the drought, but the fruit trees tried to fight, even so, there was still a mangy lemon tree with a few fruit and a stand of olives whose unremarkable foliage didn't disturb anyone and for several months Johnny just slipped into a place that had no pace. On occasions a few kangaroos came to his dam, and one day in a spectacular flourish it rained. Johnny was surprised.

He settled in, as much as anyone settles anywhere, but to the animals and the remaining indigenous people, he was visiting, but no one told him so in as many words. He only watched the evening TV news for the weather forecast, which was securely predictable. There was no one in his life he could talk to within two hundred miles, so the term 'talking to yourself' certainly applied to him, which made him chuckle as when he'd been in the city, scores of people seemed to be self circuiting themselves with headphones. For months, no one spoke, and he spoke to no one, except for the man at the shop who was the only narrator. And to blame his gradual decline was unfair on the place, as his prehistory had made him go there.

Dreams became monumental, even memorable in daylight, heat hazes became literal mirages, and another drought set in. 'Global warming' some said it was with wilful storms thrashing the east coast and inferno like bush fires down south. One day there was a smoky north wind around the town, coming from further north, but there was little to burn over there, so it didn't reach them, all of which made him anxious as there wasn't anything to do apart from watch for danger.

When in the city he had always been judgemental about other people, because in so many ways he'd become a loner, which was his way of finding himself, so he filled notebooks with details about appearances and personal scenarios. Train trips that were once enjoyable became nightmares peopled by pink hair, tattoos, gender bending, head scarves, and physical handicaps, all of which he noted. He thought his country was becoming untidy, messy and wild in ways that he hadn't been brought up to believe in because he had only ever briefly been in the bush, and the cities had become stressful. He had said that he'd write about those people, 'but too much noise got in the way', he added.

Johnny wanted to tidy up his backyard, and keep the bush under control, as he was amazed at how resilient it seemed even with little or no rain. Over the fence, there was a stretch of crown land filled with gangly gauze bushes and too many gum trees for his taste, and around town, they had popped up on the side of the road without planning permits, and there was a general wildness, usually in other people's gardens. And the long drive from the supermarket in the nearest big town became disconcerting, gum tree by gum tree insisting he see them, beckoning in their own twisted way. Around the odd corners on the highway, feral animals sometimes made a dash for cover, despite his best efforts at running them over.

On one trip to the large town after he'd been there for nearly a year, he found purpose in the hardware section of the supermarket. Against the far wall there was a clean and colourful display of whipper-snippers, trimmers, lawn mowers, and knives, practical farming tools for responsible hands. Johnny loaded up his utility truck with an assortment of tools and weapons. He found the Ute useful because loading up clippings and severed limbs into the backseat of his old Holden was silly and dirty. He drove back to his town along the highway skirting the railway line, and because it was still light the trees by the side of the road could clearly be seen, and the other natives didn't bother him.

Johnny wanted to get to work as quickly as possible. He had his old agriculture department maps of the neighbourhood with their coloured sections, and shaded areas that pinpointed clumps of trees (particularly eucalypts) and ancient watercourses, hanging up in the lounge-room, and, on another wall, a plan of action that he hoped to complete in stages.

After getting out of the Ute he nervously paced around his yard and started talking to himself. 'I'm going to cut the bush back, get rid of as many gum trees as I can, cause they love fire, and it threatens us. The greenies say that we need them, that is rubbish – we just need to have nothing that will burn, nothing that can be taken away from us – my country is under threat, and I will stop it. No one appreciates them anyway, they are always there.' As I have said, his decline was accelerating, if that is the angle you wish to contemplate it from.

Conversely, his behaviour was typically eccentric and highly individualistic, by the standards of the time, as potentially anti-social behaviour was sniggered at in the name of democracy. His impending outrage was at that stage out of sight, no one cared as it wasn't then any of their business, so they did not take offence.

Johnny grabbed his best snipper from the pile of pruning equipment. Gleefully he snipped at the shortest of the gum trees out the back, and a pile of branches began to build on the remnants of what was once a lawn prior to the long drought. He gathered strength, moving at great pace and only stopping for afternoon tea after he could see the results of his work. 'Now that is good', he thought to himself and he sat on the back step munching on biscuits and drinking water. He was pleased with his effort and made colourful Texta annotations on his map on the wall, the idea being that eventually he would fill it up.

In the heat he mused that he really wanted to bulldoze them, but, that 'trimming and pruning would have to do, that'll teach them a lesson. There will be naked trunks everywhere – and people will ask about what there was. I will clean everything up.' Over the next few weeks he methodically moved around the town and chopped away at any of the gum trees, his only two neighbours being away, so he didn't have to ask them for permission. He strode in contentment around the neighbour's yards, admiring how efficiently he had created clean, neat sections free of fallen leaves and intrusive branches.

The man in the shop noticed though, and gave him a warning, 'cut it out mate, you'll make enemies, we need them, they are our only shade, you can't see the world without some shade.' But Johnny ignored him because he had been brought up to be thorough and industrious and bright light gave him direction. Even so, he made a wider arc in his cutting, as the crown land around town was quite extensive and laden with all kinds of gums. Down the disused tracks clumps of them seemed to congregate in shallow depressions that occasionally collected water, which was their form. He was also out of sight because earlier in the week a speeding motorist noticed him hacking away in next door's front garden, which he found unnerving.

By month's end he had made progress as patches of brownie – green had disappeared from the place, and he was able to shout out loud, 'no fire will come here, just you wait and see.' No one heard him.

But people in the large town reckoned something was up. Miriam Anderson had been driving through the place one day to visit her sister in another of the tiny towns when she noticed, the cleanliness of it all, or more particularly, how things looked thinner and before long an item appeared in the local paper about a man who was taking the idea of tidy towns to an extreme, the suggestion being that he was cutting out the heart of the place to prevent its destruction. Someone was quoted as saying, 'being bushfire ready is ok, but this is ridiculous. Trees prevent erosion and provide shade.' Yet, Johnny wasn't all that worried because he was too busy stacking piles of branches and then driving them away in the Ute to another place so he didn't have to burn them there.

Eventually his two neighbours returned from where some people go to escape where they come from, and were not pleased to find sticks instead of trees in their yards, and a subsequent lack of birds and insects, so they complained to the shire council in the big town down the highway who made some inquiries with the man in the shop. The man in the shop said little as he still had the idea that people should be left alone, which was why he was there.

For several weeks, Johnny moved further out of town which was pleasing as there were plenty of helpless gums growing wild along dry creek beds and on side roads. He chopped them, trimmed them, and used a chainsaw to make them into sections, knowing he was out of sight and probably couldn't be heard. The shire council left him a letter about trespassing on other people's property, but he imagined he wouldn't hear another word from them, so he went on manically trimming, round and round in concentric circles.

The scrappy state forest to the north of the town was in his sights, and after a day's planning he had staked out the best bits for destruction, but on the morning of his first trip into what he called a wilderness, a car with the markings of the Department of Conservation and Wild Life made a U-turn towards his place in front of the shop, and a man in a green uniform came towards him. 'Unless you cease your illegal chopping, we will fine you for illegal clearing on crown land. If you continue, a jail term is possible,' the man explained, brandishing a letter above his head. 'You just can't assert yourself across everybody else.' 'But this country is mine,' Johnny replied.

Later, a car with a photographer, stopped on the highway but nothing would stop him, so for at least another month he chopped and trimmed around the outskirts of the town. 'It all looks cleaner now', he said to himself, feeling proud for once. Then, two months later a fine notice arrived in the mail, but he threw it away and kept on trimming. His case went to court in the big town and he pleaded guilty and said he wasn't subject to the law of the land and the people who were about to prosecute him were some of the villains behind the messy country he was trying to clean up. He was then sentenced to a term in the prison in the big town.

He concluded that, as it was a rebuke from officialdom he was at last vindicated, as someone doing something about the mess his country had turned into. As for the jail term he was sure he would undertake it, and it wouldn't be the end of his long decline, rather, as with many things in his country, the start of another fearful monologue.

# THE TOWN HALF WAY ACROSS AUSTRALIA

In the town half way across Australia Julius decided that he didn't want to be connected anymore. It was at one of those petrol stops, where to go on without filling up could be suicidal because there were so few towns in that part of the country. There was no one to talk to, apart from a lady in the supermarket, and even the streets were devoid of dogs in the heat.

It had been two months since he'd resigned as a communications expert in Canberra, where his mumbling and ranting became loud and embarrassing. Now, as a single man in his survival machine, he was trying to put the bastards behind him and on that highway drivers weren't comparing status because there was only the road.

Yet, he still needed to tell people things and get the message across, imagining for a moment that he might barricade the highway and ask people about their political preferences which reminded him of a friend who once published a magazine and how he delighted in leaving it at obscure towns frustrated with lack of readers in more convenient places.

The thought was a part of his madness, and an element of dedication to what had been a conscientious career. Of getting up every morning to the television news, the papers, the websites, the phone calls from his minister, and what had to be communicated that day. But he knew he was becoming clunky and unresponsive and that all the new social media devices were pushing stories further out of context, providing grabs, promoting egos, causing us to jump about like rabbits, making us more connected without being in control, while the economy ground unlucky people down.

Most mornings he had felt nauseous at the thought of another press release to write, another piece of spin to doctor. Yet for all such external demands he was essentially private, someone who needed a lot of time on his own to consider the world, not be crowded and pushed about, so it was little wonder then that he had finally come to the road.

His childhood had been a litany of bullying at the hands of a brother, of snatching precious moments of reading by torchlight after lights out, and of making up dream places in the backyard or in other vacant places. So, by the time he first went to university he was a mess with no compass to live by, ruled only by an aimlessness that could never be satisfied. Indiscriminately he started to read the entire lower floor of the library with no regard for any of his course texts and commitments.

While driving he heard an interview on ABC radio with an Australian nurse who worked in crisis management in third world countries, who made life and death decisions every day, and he knew he didn't have that kind of courage.

The town halfway across Australia was on the edge of nothing which reminded him why Canberra wasn't frightening, even if bushfires sometimes clipped the outer suburbs and heatwaves were suffocating.

This town had next to nothing and nothing seemed to reach it. On the trip over, there were campers towing tailers, the odd massive road train, a few local farmers, and backpackers in seemingly unreliable vehicles.

It was the second time he had been through the place. A month before, driving across to Perth via the Nullarbor Plain, he'd stopped for the night in the 'Best Western Motel' just off the highway as he didn't want to avoid kangaroos at night. With the best will in the world, and a dedication to the latest technology, there was no escaping how the landscape made you feel small, ineffective, and it had been a good time to daydream over his suppressed political ambitions. How in his job he had the feeling of being close to power, his prized identification tag to get into the departmental building, how he nodded in the direction of power brokers at his favourite cafe in Kingston, where people shared snippets of gossip. But he was too craggy, uncircumspect in delicate moments and something of a free spirit.

On his first trip, at another truck stop well past the shock of the treeless plain it was time to stop as his legs were aching and he was hungry. Hardly a car had passed and only a few caravans had been huddled next to sparse trees next to the road and it appeared that he was out of mobile range and internet coverage was a fiction for a communications expert.

Called Cocklebiddy, there were the usual spaces for trucks, and out the back camping facilities for campers, and a cage for budgerigars, chatting and chortling at one another. But while eating he made the mistake of glancing up at the television news and there was the same old crap coming out of Canberra.

Out of nowhere he heard 'Julius' from the direction of a battered camper van under some trees, and his first girlfriend Margaret suddenly appeared saying how she had been trying for months to track him down on Face book. Margaret was as short as he remembered, petite, but lined by time. They chatted for several hours largely about being teenagers, and she explained nervously that she was going west to east, in the opposite direction, how she was now single, that she had a daughter in Victoria to visit, and how she usually made the journey once a year in her van, 'it's the gypsy in me', she added boldly. They reminisced, but nothing happened as the highway separated them and he was hostage to his teenage memory of her, and she too was a bit broken.

Further down the road on a ninety mile flat stretch there was an emergency airstrip for the Flying Doctor Service, a few burnout and vandalised vehicles, all of which was great for cursing and ventilating, and at the next roadhouse, the girl behind the counter mentioned that she was from Estonia, and that she was enjoying the isolation from 'troubled' Europe.

Julius' mutterings were becoming stranger and stranger by the kilometre, but no one could hear and the only animals were the odd eagle and swarms of ubiquitous crows who cawed and cawed. He started reciting the best lines from his most effective press releases, and as he was alone no one could disagree. There was one he particularly remembered, really a short speech about how much a sacked minister had contributed to the nation, full of rhythmic lines and understated alliteration. 'One of my triumphs, one of my triumphs', he repeated over and over, while the car anticipated rare bends, avoided squashed kangaroos, and he noticed at least two lone bike riders struggling across the bare landscape. Was his mania repressed political or literary ambition? Either way it was becoming dangerous like driving too fast.

After the long stretch, which was only one of many, the road folded into a vast scrubby forest where there was no horizon and side roads led nowhere. Finally, another road house appeared from the scrub, this one brightly painted and staffed by another Estonian. In the yard an aboriginal woman knocked on his side window wondering whether she could get a lift into Coolgardie. She was perhaps in her forties, seemed lost and very strange to Julius who had been used to writing press releases about indigenous issues, rather than talking to any aborigines. It was a junction of the east/west and north/south highways, and as there weren't any trains, backpackers also congregated, so he said yes, and for the entire ninety or so kilometres she hardly said a word, only that she was going to see her mob. Julius imagined that she was frightened of him, as he of her.

After Coolgardie the road veered south west past spooky salt lakes but there were patches of reasonably tall gums and side roads to mine sites. Utility trucks with bobbing flags and flashing lights on top made up most of the traffic, and slowly there were signs of past habitation, crumbling stone cottages and futile attempts at gardens, but gradually the country took on a different shape as fields appeared with wheat and a few sheep and there were mail boxes on the highway. After travelling most of the day he could see Perth at last in the distance, the tall buildings of the city centre, aeroplanes like moving shadows in the sky and reflections off the sea.

He had the address of an old acquaintance from Melbourne who lived quite close to Fremantle where he could stay a few nights as there was nowhere further west.

But there was something about Fremantle that drove him completely crazy, how it foisted its heritage of old buildings onto a sprawling city, and how the people in the cafes seemed disdainful of those who visited on weekends. They were posing behind laptops and overly expensive breakfasts, in between strutting about on their mobile phones and some had fashionable beards. He imagined they were arty types. 'Frustrated wankers', he muttered. Yet for all that it looked like the suburb was crumbling, scrappy, pleading for itself, surrounded by growing strata title estates and burgeoning freeways. 'They are smug', he thought, 'they know that it is all bullshit and bluster. That's why they pretend not to care for all that communications crap, why my old job was important. Why they don't care about the cost to me, and why I came all this way.'

It was of course unfair to people he hadn't really met, circumspect and grotesque, but the trip had, it seemed, flattened out his finer nuances, but it should also be said that that wasn't just the fault of the highway and an horizon that lacked resolve, it was the PR crap in Canberra, and everywhere else, that had moulded and massaged his vaulting and shrivelled ego.

He tried to strike up conversations with strangers, but unlike back on the highway you couldn't ask people about their precise destination and any events on their journey so far, so they stuttered, apologized and scrambled for phrases. There were a few erudite people, fond of their own words, in ways that were indulgent and definitely inefficient as communication, he concluded. He wanted to be a bit like them, but that might be messy and unstructured, the very elements he avoided so as to get to where he had been. He decided to stay for a least a week and made arrangements with a boarding house in one of the raffish, but rundown streets close to the harbour, but it was full of other migrants from sensible Australia, ageing hippies, relatively homeless youths, and some backpackers, who at least knew they were moving on. His friend from the old days had found Julius increasingly strange and perverse, especially when conversations were heated and Julius became repetitive and his wandering the streets late at night unnerved his two young children. So Julius had moved out.

Julius couldn't read books because the stories in his head screamed and wouldn't allow in any others, so staying in the boarding house was stifling. Dressed in the same black pants and tee shirt he walked the streets day and night, normally when there were preening and purposeful people in the coffee shops, imaging that he might link up with someone who might understand his thoughts on how public relations was destroying Australia. But really there was no one as most people thought it very strange engaging in impromptu conversations about such serious subjects when all they wanted was to be left alone.

So he became a joke, a tourist attraction, and an entertaining moment in a place screaming out for authenticity. There were also nasty people who said he was creepy.

He was continually talking, mumbling and then shouting at the top of his voice the best lines from his best press releases, particularly phrases that caught the moment and the baristas waved and called out his name, complimenting him on what they said was his repertoire. It was almost as though he was singing as the lines crashed into one other, but he couldn't be caught by anyone who wanted to chat as on and on he walked until finally he must have exhausted himself, but no one knew where he'd gone. Like many of us, he had no name as such (that anyone could recall), so his eccentricity never made it in the papers, and he was too scatty for TV.

The police were pretty tolerant as they only ever checked him over when he bothered the girls at McDonalds with rhetorical inquiries about the different choices on the menu, and they knew he wasn't a criminal, didn't deal in drugs, and probably just needed a good bath. So Julius didn't achieve the kind of notoriety needed in those days, he was non-violent, so not a threat, and he really wasn't funny enough to be a good performer, so he had to move on.

* * *

The thought of Canberra nauseated him, and the idea of another drive across the treeless plain seemed then too much even in his few slow moments of reflection, but he couldn't stay in the west. He had got away for sure, but he knew he'd become worse despite the distance. He took an alternate route on the way back, down through some forests and greener country to the south and in that way the highway eluded him. At Esperance the sight of the sea was enough to lift his spirits. There were fishermen, and relaxed locals shopping. Eventually though he had to go north up to the highway which he met at Norseman. The long stretches started again, with the ubiquitous crows and burnt out car bodies and he couldn't get across it fast enough. He wasn't home, even though he was an Australian. It was not his country.

The road tossed and teased him and he knew again that he didn't have anyone to talk to. On long stretches he could see an ex colleague in Canberra scurrying about his office, one hand on his mobile, the rest of his body sprawled in front of his computer. People were milling about discussing the latest angle coming out of the minister's office, their identification tags visible. He'd been there once and revelled in it, his ex-wife treating him with respect as he had status for once. He walked taller in those days even though he was broken or perceptive, depending on your perspective. He had 'cracked' as it were after a long night with colleagues at a restaurant in Kingston. It was a rollicky and irreverent night, egos crashing, promotions in the wind, of which he wanted one, and the colleague that he could now recall saying, 'You know it is all a game.' After that Julius' output and press releases lost their edge, he couldn't control his grammar and his sarcasm became melancholic.

A bend in the road jolted him awake and a road train thundered out of the horizon and it was time to concentrate the mind on next to nothing. Roadhouses flew by, monstrous cliffs dropped into the sea a few kilometres off the road and there was an aboriginal community with its own gate and made road to the left. A forest of scrubby eucalypts went on for miles until finally signs of European habitation appeared, windmills, fence lines, and a water pipeline with graffiti scrawled across it about other journeys and trysts. Gradually, the country returned to wheat fields and the sight of families driving into town. But Julius had no one to talk to and if he went back to Canberra it would just mean driving aimlessly around to see if his former colleagues were home and then they would be even more wary of him.

Finally he made it into the town half way across Australia. The highway still went through the main street so there some people coming and going into typical shops such as a supermarket, a pharmacy, a post office, a second-hand shop, and next to the only bank, an animal shelter run by Beryl who was nice and talkative the locals said, but there was little that was romantic about the place. If you half closed your eyes you might imagine that the town never ended, only petered out in unplanned sheds and machinery yards.

Beryl took in injured animals, mainly kangaroos, wombats, and even the odd emu. Julius recalled seeing her yellow rescue van on the highway punctuated by road kill, the first time he'd driven across it. This time Beryl was in town in her office surrounded by cages with cockies and bandaged wombats and middle-aged women drinking tea.

Enquiring in town about accommodation he mumbled and there was fear in his eyes and he didn't know how long he would be staying and why. They had seen people like him as the town was a stopover across the continent; in any case, there was a small cottage up on Clarke's road that needed a tenant, so he decided to stay for a bit.

The next day he walked into Beryl's animal shelter where injured kangaroos gazed at him with gooey eyes, there was a winged tailed eagle, and a few limping dogs demanding her attention and he said, 'I've got no one to talk to.' She smiled and said, 'You are in the right place then', and suggested that he come in and see how he went with the animals.

At first his crazy speech spooked the dogs and the eagle looked like it wanted to bite his ear off, anyhow, the wombats and the kangaroos couldn't care less and were soothing in non committal ways, and after a while, one of the recovering Labradors insisted on walking with him back and forth to his place.

# THE SWEET SPOT

Walter reckoned the trouble was that everyone was looking the wrong way in their search for the real Australia. There was the famous painter who encouraged his thinking by concentrating on still objects in a seemingly static landscape, and a novelist in Victoria whose subjects always shimmered, and who asked questions about the nature of memory and was deliberately tricky about it.

Walter was dissatisfied as all hell, as he had seen it all before, the endless quest for authenticity and new perspectives built over the old. Surely, he pondered, somewhere there must be a sweet spot of some sort that might energize everything, and be able to suck in desires, fears and memories. He would go in search of it, no matter what it took to track it down. It could be more than any place; maybe a mood or in an emblem. The problem in the past was that we were actively in search of it, when we didn't really want to be. But it might be right in front of our noses.

Walter thought that it might be found in short stories in a country known for wise cracks and unsaid things, as novels, in his view, were often long-winded ego trips, involving characters who talked too much and Australia had quite a few of those. The rest of the media could only cope with static images like wine, beaches, and the outback. Some had suggested Australia was a sweeping landscape, of heroic failures and ordinary optimism, but he doubted it. 'It's more like an old adolescent', he often shouted at anyone who could hear. 'Why do we patronize ourselves so much? Why are we colonials' deep inside out heads?' That though seemed too simple and abrupt for people who often liked being peasants.

What had got him going was the sight of another arts festival full of promotional language like, 'international and internationally renowned artists' in his home state which still wanted to be a part of England, and at the back of it all, the telly was ruled by the lives of Americans. Walter was a struggling musician and it was very hard to get airplay and space for live gigs, but he was energetic and very cranky.

Walter was wild, as much as anyone could be in such a still place, and he began to drive and drive to try and find the sweet spot. There was no need for a long road trip as that was too conventional like the first explorers and he wasn't like Jack Kerouac in search of America.

The artist he admired, had it seemed, found his spot by leaving for Europe and then painting places across all that distance, by putting it behind him in the search for excellence. A friend who used to paint, but doubted he had that level of technique, and was still in awe of the old masters, suggested we live in a cultural desert, which hardly helped to alleviate Walter's mood.

So he went in search, at first, for tactile things, like the famous artist, all over the city as the countryside had been covered and wasn't yet a home for non-indigenous Australians. Some people used their cars as symbols, the Ford and Holden drivers who drove like maniacs, pretending that they were racing drivers along suburban streets, some displayed the national flag like an upturned thumb from roofs, and some had witty sayings on rear windows and boots. But Walter had a sign made up which said, 'honk if you can take me to your Australian sweet spot', knowing full well that smart arses would want to tell him about their g spots.

On his first trip he drove aimlessly across the northern suburbs of the city, up and down streets that didn't go anywhere much, as they repeated themselves in their sameness. Further out from the suburbs he found semi industrial estates with vacant lots that had a few horses munching stoically on dry grass, with for sale signs that stressed possible commercial developments that really weren't there in an ailing economy. Yet he did have a moment alongside a vacant lot that suggested views of the blue ranges beyond a housing estate where half closing his eyes he thought he saw the sight of an Eden smudged by an image of money on one side of the frame. But he drove on unable to find anything definitive, or where any blood might rush to his head, but of course that was an opportunistic way to go about creativity.

But his adventures started on his way back. Cars started honking and people were hanging out of windows skylarking, cracking jokes and being like the larrikins they had heard about on the television or at school. Some asked him to stop and then suggested that he follow them to their sweet spot, or they kindly gave him directions to a place that was a best kept secret.

But before long a lady with two grandchildren insisted that she knew her sweet spot. 'I will take you to my local beach. You can gaze away to other places. It is a lovely place, you wouldn't want to be anywhere else, but I always think of more interesting places when I am there,' which reminded Walter of a time in Queensland where a woman snapped at a poetry reading that 'This place isn't a site for culture,' after one of the speakers made the claim that the Gold Coast was a place to study where Australian's pursued pleasure. She looked desperate like all snobs do.

He was about to return home when two rough guys in a panel van almost forced him off the road. Without giving their names they almost spoke together, partly completing sentences in such a way as to make it clear that they were a combination of comedians and gangsters. The van had etchings of naked women on the bonnet and a dark interior with mauve couches and what looked like some gym equipment. The taller of the two announced, 'Mate, what it is with you? What's the bloody sign supposed to mean? Anyway, we'll show you what we reckon is our sweet spot. See inside, that's where we sometimes bash black people on Friday and Saturday nights, and anyone else who's not like us, can get a turn, if they are really unlucky.' Walter started to back away, but they drove off pleased it seemed that they had made some noise.

The news spread about Walter's quest, partly of course because it was crazy and obviously a bit quirky. The local paper ran an article on him and asked why he was all fired up, but when the interview turned to any political theory he might have as to his thinking, the reporter said that he couldn't reduce all his words to anything ordinary people might understand, so the piece was very short. Even so, people sought out his car down at the shops and honked whenever they saw him. Of course there were by then the usual sky-larkers, but even in that Walter felt vindicated as those moments were perhaps part of a pattern. He wondered what that famous painter would have thought sitting in a paddock with an old farm house in front of him where things were still.

The next day he received a phone call from a woman who introduced herself as the secretary of the Bi Bin Country Women's Association asking him whether he'd be interested in coming up for afternoon tea. It was close to the city so he said he'd be delighted. She added, 'We think we live in a sweet spot', and then chuckled. 'See what you think, you obviously have a sense of humour young man.' So he drove up. It wasn't much of a place, but that made the mind see different things, he thought. Without traffic you could see children laughing and playing, and also signs of poverty in ramshackle houses and old cars. As events were moving so quickly Walter didn't have time to keep a journal, but he would have written something along the lines of,

> *It was a truly beautiful afternoon, the ladies put on what they called a spread, of cakes, scones, jam and cream. They were friendly, and asked me why I was going about my search, and there was a little evidence of town gossip. They all made a claim that their meeting room was in the very centre of Australia. The secretary Jane was remarkable, as she left me as I got into my car with the words, 'You know Australian's are only proud one day of the year because they don't really believe in themselves. They are a bit like my nephews, they haven't grown up yet. And this from a monarchist! Perhaps they more fully understand peasants. It was a strange day.*

The article in the local paper also connected Walter with intrigued educational institutions, because in those days if things happened in the media they were actually happening. Such events weren't just the idle fancies of ordinary people for once.

A group of polite students from one of the better schools in the city contacted Walter intrigued at what they called his 'radical' action of inviting everyday people in suggesting their own sweet spots. They were also in year twelve where the history teacher had suggested that events in history are made up of a myriad of individual perceptions (which was pretty radical in his workplace) and there were also a few students enrolled in a cross-disciplinary unit called 'Imagining Australia'. So Walter went to the school in a leafy suburb adjacent to a large park, where the students (boys and girls) were all dressed in immaculate uniforms, feeling like an imposter, and they said they also knew about sweet spots. The teacher said that they'd do an assignment on the idea as long as it was serious and wasn't just about sex.

On his way back home, he inadvertently packed his car in a back lane behind a large restaurant in the city, as he had forgotten the address where he was to meet a friend and stumbled into a grimy kitchen staffed by a crowd of casual workers. Further down the lane there was a faded sign on a building called The Workers' Memorial replete with peeling exhortations to the old eight-hour day and a minimum wage, all of which looked ancient.

He was nearly home when a car full of boisterous boys, in cricket whites, drew level at the lights, waving bats, calling and pointing at them, 'sweet spot, sweet spot'. They sped off down the road, to their match reminding him of how many ovals were in play that day.

The next morning, rounding a bend in another suburban street a man gestured to him to stop. He was towing a trailer with a few sheep. Introducing himself as Nick, he said that he could show him where a sweet spot was, 'Mate come with me to my hobby farm up in the hills, I've got a mob of sheep that I care for.'

So they drove up past an endless row of car yards, Woolworth's stores, and convenience shops until finally, after negotiating a twisting road and a town with antique shops, Nick took him into a pleasant property and the sound of sheep and birds. Nick leaned on a gate and announced, 'this might be what you are looking for in your search – sheep'. Nick, a retired school teacher had got the serious joke behind

Walter's lament, and it seemed he was quite erudite. 'See them, they aren't threatening and quite cuddly especially the lambs, we love them, but for centuries now we have grazed and gazed at them, but they are stupid. They like paddocks and they run at odd angles when asked to go in any direction. Their weakness is their strength. Could they be a bit like us?'

Nick could see the madness in Walter's search, how any place is a mess of particular insights, angles and oddities, and that we largely only see ourselves as individuals, but he could relax. Walter though had to keep on looking.

# SPOTTING

When Sheldon said that he likes trains on the telly, William finally felt good. Sheldon was famous you see, and William was nobody. It was just that some people thought his relentless train trips were a waste, up and down to town several times a day, and for something of a relief, the longish journey to the sea or up to the port.

Without work he wanted to keep busy and methodical. Detailed maps of the suburban lines were spread out on his kitchen table, kept in place by empty vegemite jars, and as it was a compact city, excursions were meticulously planned out in his head because one could travel there and back to the end of any line in a day.

The information board of coming and going trains was like a lolly shop, as it had precise possibilities, and an excitement only measured by his need for organization. He clapped his hands and jumped up and down in anticipation on the platform.

His collection of mint timetables was one of his treasures, which he hunted down on hearing that they had just been published and his trips a chance to clear out the people in his head. As a rule, he spoke to no one and no one spoke to him.

He didn't live far from his local station so he heard the reassuring whirring of the passenger diesels every morning and night. His flat was modest, and as he slept alone he was kept company by what he called his Byda, a neat piece of rag from childhood, which he couldn't get to sleep without because it was something to touch and would always be there.

At his station there were school children every morning, joking and larking about with their school bags, and in winter, crest fallen office workers scrolling their mobile phones, plus a few local football supporters wrapped in distinctive scarves.

He planned everything such as the place where he got onto the train, just up from the few seats on the platform, fifteen feet from where the pedestrian bridge finished. It was possible to travel all day on one ticket so long as he changed trains in the city, and everything became familiar, houses that had been there for a hundred years, the same disabled people in wheelchairs, the old Greek lady with her trolley and the tattooed man who once told William that he got all of them done so that he could hide from people.

Trains had tracks and went in one direction, whereas cars were like animals darting off at angles and sometimes crashing into things and he was able to recognise people because there weren't many about in that compact city.

But he had a special destination, and therefore a favourite trip every week, to his mother's grave in a tidy cemetery on the banks of a river that only flowed in winter, up at the end of the northern line, in an old town that was starting to look like an outer suburb. Meryl died twenty years before (he never knew his father), and her cooking and cleaning for him stopped. He finally went on the pension when a social worker reported that she thought he'd finally become unstable and overly introverted, and he probably couldn't ever hold down a job or withstand the stress of study, something they'd first suggested at school.

The cemetery was only a few streets from the railway station, which was next to Coles, not far from the river. He would replenish any dying flowers, and in case anyone was watching, shyly place a note on the headstone.

William made sure that he would go there every Thursday afternoon after his short spurts into stations at inner suburbs and beach locations where he'd order fish and chips at the local take-aways. Knowing each route by heart he knew there was always an interesting thing about all places, and occasionally, in unplanned ways, the railways sometimes used old rolling stock on his line. Those old trains came out of the big bend and under the pedestrian bridge into his station. They had cushiony seats and distinct compartments, vinyl panelling, and discreet spaces and they accelerated much slower than the new trains. The office workers could relax; the school children had room for card games, laptops, and gossip.

If William had any heroes, apart from a few people on the telly, it was the train drivers who he greeted in his cryptic way at the central station as they were known to him and him to them. Peter, who usually drove on one of the beach lines, was always friendly because William was at least a 'satisfied customer,' he told his mates, 'unlike the crazy druggies and miserable geriatrics who clamber on and off every day.' He too, loved trains, knowing full well that people took them for granted, didn't care for their history and idolized cars. William was devoid of such words, but he would have agreed in his own way.

At the central station people always seemed to be rushing, even in the middle of the day, especially if they were late for work or an appointment, but William loved the hold-ups as long as they weren't too disruptive, marking off any unusual movement in an exercise book, which became highlights when he returned home at the end of the day. 'The Seaford line timetable will have to be changed', he would tell any of the inspectors he could find before leaving.

William was 'simple', people said; some sniggered, but not those who secretly wished they could be more like him.

# IRONY

Derrick had so much irony in him he decided one morning to try to get rid of some of it by swimming in the sea. It was at his usual place, not that many of his friends ever went there, as it was too viscous a location, they would say because it wouldn't bend to them. But Derrick was overwhelmed by his history and needed to get rid of some of it. Like most things that swim was a paradox, as it's hard to be sarcastic about seagulls and the odd dolphin. He'd been going there for years, even in cold weather he found it a place where he could be still.

There was irony, irony everywhere, everyone was referring to something else, someone else; there was a half-arsed theory for everything, and his years at university had got him all twisted instead of enlightened, even though he wanted to say something.

Where he swam stayed the same through all seasons, except for the temperature and the tides. The rumour was that a man with no story had died there, up in the sand-dunes several years before after camping out for months in a sheltered spot. The threads of the story went this way – the man was slightly handicapped, he had no place to go, and there weren't any other homeless people around. The police kept an eye on him. The elderly couple who picked up garbage on the beach most mornings noticed his used cans and junk on the side of one of the sand dunes, and he never had a funeral, and being a skimpy story, they made it up, without too much explanation.

The place was also notable for big sunsets, a haze like horizon where nothing was certain, and it was close to where his parents had moved to years before, so that they too could sometimes go and see the sea. Going there he tried to see patterns, and there were shapes unlike in his writing where he tried to put everything in, which made him sick instead of kind, something that had been building up and up in a frenetic and hopeless search for the new. There was always more to the story as it was with an acquaintance whose poetry contained impressive references to other poets. But he was always unsatisfied.

Derrick had decided to write a story about his old dog, even though friends sniggered at him, saying, 'Where's the irony in that? About just one dog, why not all dogs?' In any case Derrick had made up his mind, and there was a first line and a kind of coda which went – 'Of course I am not being sentimental', which he imagined might play into the hands of the experts in irony.

One hot day at the beach he was hallucinating. From a distance it seemed as if a small boat had turned over in the swell beyond the breakwater. It was a high tide as the moon had been full the night before, but he could see what looked like piles of paper washing up on the sand. He saw that the paper consisted of articles on the use of dogs in literature, reams of it, from important sounding journals that specialised in the study of experimental writing. He felt hot, and for a good amount of time, his idea of his dog disappeared from view – 'I can't do that, I just can't do it', he muttered as children and other dogs splashed about.

It would though be foolish to suggest that he wanted to be safe in his ignorance as he'd been an ardent visitor to a bookshop in the city that specialised in irony, references to everything else and which had regular ironical installations with long winded catalogue essays. People would stand around, particularly after poetry readings and suggest how there might be ironical significance in this and that; that, the last poem was elusive and shard like. There, culture was about anointing people, unlike with his family, with whom he felt dutiful and small. Derrick just wanted to read the start of his story.

One of the reasons for his new direction (as if anyone could find such a thing in those days) was the difficulty he had with girls. He had been trying hard to be ironic, or humorous in clever ways, imagining that that was what they liked, instead of toned bodies, but he was of course reaching too much for an outline, and individual differences slid away.

He told people he liked the US show 'Big Bang Theory' but the problem was that some friends said it was popular and therefore it couldn't be ironic, and there was a problem with some of the humour as it bordered on being stereotypical they said. Some girls told him that about the women in the show. Penny for example was sexually constructed, but Derrick just saw her as the no nonsense figure. So it was slippery in those days as everyone had their own ironic agenda, which seemed funny at first but could be really devious underneath.

Derrick quite enjoyed his swim and he left the water feeling lighter, with a new resolve to tackle his irony. It had been a badly ironical month, his so called best friend Robert was in a bad way as he'd enrolled in a creative writing class full of what he called 'sincere no talents', many straight out of school, who had no interest in philosophy he said, but they knew about irony in popular culture – the Simpsons and all that, and all the wacky celebrities, which Robert thought made them trivial. They also knew that they could be working in hospitality for many years, despite university degrees, and there was irony in that.

Robert you see once told his tutor that he was going to write 'the perfect story' which could eliminate human mess. He said it was be a quasi-mathematical formula that would take account of all points of view, character traits and unbelievable moments, and he was astonished that the tutor was astonished, and after that he became depressed and angry about the others in the class.

So, Derrick decided to take him to his part of the untidy sea and they walked along the foreshore and said little which only made Robert worse. Robert had been reading copious books on photographic theory and how the lens of the camera was often dictatorial, and been going to ironic installations at the bookshop about light and colour, so he saw the seagulls as nuisances, and that dolphins were engaged in attention seeking behaviour.

Irony was everywhere and Derrick just had to go for another swim as his dog story gnawed at him and starred in his dreams. Robert wanted to be brilliant and hated how it was that some in his class loved it when one guy, Warwick read his emotional stories which he religiously called a kind of realism. To Robert he was vulgar and uninformed, fancy writing stories without knowing all the permutations of the term. Warwick was a wrecking ball lacking in irony, he decided in a vulgar moment. He would turn up to seminars in gym shorts and tees shirts and burrow into other people's work like an animal and say that there was too much irony about, how he loved the masculinity of Ernest Hemingway and the gravitas of Herman Melville's sea sagas.

Out to sea in the swell, container ships were queuing to go into the port way out of sight to the right of the sand dunes, there was a clear line to where the tide had receded overnight, and birds were dive bombing for fish in the shallows. A few people were having what appeared to be animated discussions on their mobile phones and dogs were paddling about. Behind all of that some people were talking and living irony, chatting away in person and on-line, there was the buzz of regular traffic and someone was shouting.

Derrick was at last feeling better after another swim, and Robert even sat for a time on the sand and noticed how the waves came in and then pushed back against themselves. He admitted then, with tears in his eyes, that he just didn't like other people and, after a pause sneakily told Derrick, 'You know there is something pure and simple in this contradiction at my feet.'

# GOING IT ALONE

What would you do if you desperately wanted to change things but most people just couldn't care less? That is the question Alice pondered every morning on her way to work as a clinical psychologist, surrounded by what looked like an epidemic of depression all around her. Every second person was writing a fantasy novel. How much of the depression was social and how much of it clinical?

On the way to her air-conditioned office above the city, she usually came across an elderly man selling the *Left Weekly* on the railway station steps, and although quite sympathetic she tried to avoid him, to refrain from reading the headline for that day: things like 'The reef at risk from capitalist miners', or, 'Abbot's Islamophobia'.

In winter she always dwelt on underlying themes, others read gossip magazines and perused Instagram for humorous cat videos, but not Alice. Another question was always, 'is the major political problem these days fundamentalism?' But, she was taught, to concentrate on individual problems and was instinctively caring and considerate and broad issues were sometimes tiresome, but she couldn't get the sight of refugee children out of her head. Her mother was sick again, living in a home a fair distance away, with indications of dementia. As the only daughter she felt responsible, as her brothers, would only make pronouncements about what needed to be done. There were always little things to do.

When she had to go over to meetings at the university she noticed that, for the first time in years, there was a strong radical student presence on campus. The international socialists of Trotskyite persuasion were highly organized and sold their publications and newspapers from trestle tables in the quadrangle, and accosted people like her about cuts to university funding. They were passionate and enthusiastic in their own way, full of hope, even if they only highlighted what they opposed and seemed naive and opportunistic to many. Their fierce flame always flickered.

In the face of their entreaties she felt guilty, even though her record of past political action was quite intact. She had written some books, but her practicality, and caring instincts, always wrestled with whether writing was too slow in a world where things changed so rapidly, and there were members of the student group who would have agreed.

The socialists were the only ones protesting among a myriad of fresh, young faces most of whom just wanted to get through, perhaps get jobs, and lead 'cool' lives. One student stood out, Richard, who she had seen for years in and around the place. He was tall, aquiline, with longish hair, and in dim light might even be mistaken for a sepia image of Jesus. The students respected his intelligence and passion; there was much to be admired.

Alice liked to see herself as something of a larrikin with a quick wit, which was her way of dealing with the absurdity of life; in fact she knew it was her way of coping. She often felt that she should be more demur, as the ladylike tag was central to her conditioning and some friends were a little critical of her exuberant, satirical outbursts. Inevitably of course, she stumbled on people, who had little or no sense of humour, and absurd moments became awkward, but most people could see the difference.

One day when she had a quarter an hour to spare on her way to a symposium with the university human services people, she perused the titles on the socialist table, concluding that they were too serious, and maybe 'too one dimensional', a touch too evangelical and sanctimonious, she quipped to her comfortable self.

She was a cocky in her cage, and the exchange with two of the students became grotesque, suggesting as she did, that there should be a Trot joke book. 'Alight then', the student said, 'give me a joke'.

Alice was slightly taken a back with the possibility that a Trot might have a sense of fun, but she ploughed on. 'Ok', Alice replied, gulping at the demand, and coming up with a line or two from the top of her head. 'What is the difference between Mormons and Trots?' 'What?' the student said. 'Mormons have American accents', Alice replied, beaming through a smart arse expression after which she left, and they chuckled, perhaps at Alice, probably at the joke, most likely thinking that the exchange was odd coming from such a person. Perhaps it was her way of interrogating sanctimonious behaviour as even her 'cool' friends with progressive views seemed safe in their marginal enclaves and disdainful of more fractious, incomplete people. She also had a list of perversely perceptive jokes about what she called 'hippy' and 'hipster' snobs.

But it wasn't a level playing field as she had had a religious upbringing which she could bring to her take on society; years of rhetorical experience and ethical dilemmas. An uncle had been a missionary among the natives in Bolivia for over thirteen years, and she had living relatives who followed him into the field, living compassionate or deluded lives, depending on the angle you constructed it. Childhood then was a slide show of reflected black and white images, of other people's struggle, with wisdom older and distant.

Her relatives weren't typically fundamentalist in their beliefs, but its ghost could often be heard in the certainties of their speech, and the church was a large organization, with property and buildings to its name, unlike the more isolated sects, who preached extremism.

She had been to Sunday school all the years of her childhood. Looking back she noticed how there was also a sense of joy and community. Her mother dutifully sat in one of the pews, and at home waited for her father to come home. No stumping on street corners for them, yet it was built on a kind of sacrifice, of relatives who when overseas did it tough. Perhaps then, the comparisons with the Trotskyite International Socialists were trite, she tentatively mused as she wandered off to her meeting.

The Trots had to gather supporters wherever they could. They saw a great capitalist conspiracy cornering them out of the media, misusing their words and actions, no matter what they did, making compromise an evil in itself. Richard certainly saw it that way, but he was charming, and read Marxism in strict ways, like others read the Bible. Always in the morning he had another issue to have a position on, another meeting to organize, and across the campus, scores of potential converts to their way of seeing the world. To proselytize was a hard road, in the new information age, as so many causes were visible, and on every street corner in the city there was someone asking for something and the last thing many people wanted was serious issues after a long day in crushing jobs.

Yet Alice admired Richard's determination when other people were looking after themselves. What kind of sacrifice was he making? She could see the parallels with the protests against the Vietnam war, and from what she had found out, a small minority were trying to gather more supporters, but this time the trade unions were increasingly powerless, and the working class dispersed, unemployed, fractured and an image of the past, even though the Trots spoke of them romantically.

Alice had heard of the anti-war students at her first university some years before she attended, strident and confident and the fear in the hearts of the government of the time. Maybe it would happen again now as the economy was weakening, but far flung right wing groups were trying to frighten un-political people and racism was visible in Australia. Islamic state was bombing everywhere overseas but because of television it hit home. The 'conditions', she thought were too different as a human services expert was prattling on about how to engage employees. A part of her was ashamed that she was thinking about history when technocrats were trying to obliterate different ideas, and there was talk that a few lecturers needed to be monitored because they were sounding too 'socialist'. One of the anthropology lecturers even told the meeting of a dream about a male history lecturer stealing her research findings. Alice began wondering what Richard might be doing.

The meeting ended, petered out, with no conclusions to speak of, but the participants seemed positive about the lack of resolution and the buzz words. They were in tune with the tenor of the times, where being in the moment was enough, because little could be grasped.

Alice had read how after the US defeat in Vietnam in 1975 when ex-radicals had the idea that they could change society by infiltrating the institutions. But on this morning she was glad she had a job and a suite of believable ideas, only that she was again disconcerted so little had changed since then.

She returned to her office, a stream of emails waiting, several texts and evidence of activity on her social media account. There is action, she concluded, how much of it is reaction? The terrorism debate seemed like ping pong and both sides were making themselves up by being different. There was too much noise and terrible violence.

Alice had been in the job for over a decade and she had worked very hard to get there, years of postgraduate study, meticulous job applications, and wrestling with self doubt, and sexism in some workplaces. She was independent she concluded, a woman in her own right which made her attractive to others. Her love life was stimulating, but somewhat one-dimensional, according to a few close women friends, and long-term relationships were in the past, and so was children.

She had a profile on social media, a list of interests and socially aware causes she was interested in, and a sense of self which she theorised was more significant than many other consumers and she could agree with like-minded people without being challenged to consider different opinions. Connected like never before, she knew that it didn't mean she had more control.

All in all, she worried about effectiveness because some things cut very deeply, like one of her brothers who often said, 'What a wank', in his typically brutal way from his part of the engine room of capitalism. 'Sis is just being a girl', he often said to his long-suffering wife whenever Alice came around and talked. Status was all too often a thin consolation. Where was the great fracturing moment that might change the way power was handed out? And how do we know when we have changed anything? Feminism for her wasn't the only answer. Where was the wonder and stupid enthusiasm of youth?

Richard had finally finished his degree even though everything he'd been taught seemed trite to his mind. The other undergraduates seemed to him naive and passive, even if quite sane given what was going on in the world. They seemed unfazed, quick and mobile and trained to grasp the moment. Richard's high profile professional parents had given him the ability to slice through dross and see any of the underlying patterns, so it was no wonder that he found Marx satisfying as an explanation for the broad sweep of history, and of any of the underlying structures. But he was also often too quick in his conclusions; some might say it was arrogance, but to his group of Trots, it was charming and inspirational, as they knew his involvement was another sacrifice. They mixed socially as there wasn't any difference between the private and the political, relationships blossoming then petering out perhaps because love was broadly seen as a bourgeois thing. The world of uncommitted people was out there, and to relax about the work needed to be done, made him mad.

He had often seen Alice in the city or around the university, her hair bobbing up and down as she walked. Her quips, he knew, covered up a deep disquiet, but she had a history of social involvement and shouldn't be discounted, so he always made a bee line toward her when selling their latest paper for at least she would buy one. Whether he thought her cute, despite the age difference, his busy demeanour would not betray. Broadly, love was an unnecessary sentiment. But he did notice how Alice had pretty green-grey eyes and shapely legs. She in turn saw a likeness in him to her late uncle in the way he attracted followers, and his quiet and steely determination was opposite to her need to vent, so she made sure that she frequented the places he would go. The pub after demonstrations, even though he was surrounded by people with banners and signs, even if her friends thought she was being stupid, needy and conventional.

The Trot group gained energy from their opposition and during that time the Reclaim Australia Party were trying to close down mosques and generally create mayhem. In her small city they organized some rallies after there had been isolated acts of terrorism, and finally the group could see what they were up against – hard men like cage fighters shouting obscenities against all Arabs everywhere, and impoverished victims of economic rationalism yelling about what they saw as *their* Australia.

One Sunday Alice made it to the place where the anti-racism alliance faced off against the opposition crowd, Richard fearlessly at the front, directing an amazing array of chants, and later in the pub, among the sweat and the adrenalin, she made the point of praising him as she was tired of being rational, professional, and unemotional, dismissing that the event gave publicity to their opposition, and could be a series of shadows and that the students saw their performance as a political act. They had asked a student from Iraq to speak at the counter rally, but she declined, saying she didn't want to be a token object.

Month by month Alice was noticing how 'realistic' her colleagues at work were becoming to protect their jobs and the illusion that they were independent. Such was the nature of political difference in those days, but to stand aside was cute and safe, even though each side made up the other side of the whole depressing story and friends were saying to her, 'don't lose control of yourself'. But she had also attended a seminar on data retention and surveillance which descended into a debate about whose rights were the most important to protect in such a dangerous world, after which she raced across town to find out where Richard was. Donald Trump was also making her mad.

In a crazy way, she was still convinced that there was a secret co-operative story, that's if anyone could survive for long enough among the tight little frames set up by popular ones.

Alice decided that her story should be inconveniently conventional as she was pissed off with most people's lack of commitment and what the clinical psychologist in her called 'recreational grieving'. So she decided that she would try to love Richard, and he would love her in return.

# GRIEF

*though they sink through the sea, they shall rise again*
*though lovers be lost, love shall not*
*And death shall have no dominion ...*

Dylan Thomas, 1933

Alice's work was often confronting, which was the last thing she needed after seeing the television news first thing in the morning. Hardly a week went by without another crazy mass bombing somewhere decimating the lives of innocent people. It made her jittery, grumpy and sometimes short-tempered. In her office, five floors up and away from the increasing number of beggars at street level, she was perusing a folder containing case file details of five individuals (called clients), who'd been detained and admitted for observation to the psychiatric ward at Bayside hospital.

Each of them had behaved in ways that the police and doctors considered was a danger to themselves and perhaps to others. As a clinical psychologist she'd been asked to ascertain the fine line between obsession and illness, if there existed anything that was clinical and needed to be referred on to a psychiatrist. But as the crazy nature of politics persisted, she knew that there'd be some difficulty in doing that. The dilemma reminded her of a rich relative, who because he had money, behaved in anti-social ways and got away with it. These people she noticed, at first glance, weren't like him.

The bulging yellow folder sat on top of her desk. She had already met each of them individually where they had been quiet and co-operative. There was to be a follow-up meeting involving all of them at Bayside just after lunch, and she noticed two common themes: they were all male and each was obsessive in some way.

Each person, she wondered, wasn't dangerous as such, but they were seriously irritating to others. Walter, a man in his early thirties, was picked up by the police as he manically drove through the suburbs with his 'show me your sweet spot' sign and came under notice as a possible stalker, according to a woman from Campbelltown. Beneath a veneer of tolerance and difference, there was always a fear about individual security, and Walter was, it seemed, too open to other people with his desire to find their 'sweet spots', which had outraged the woman in the first place with what she saw as its sexual connotations. After questioning by the police he, 'became angry and ultra-defensive and resisted arrest', the file said.

Further into the folder, there was the case of William, who was taken into custody after resisting efforts to leave the last train on the Seaford line the week before. It was estimated that was in his early forties. The ticket inspectors, knew him as a simple man and a regular traveller, who was never aggressive, but on that night, something had set him off, and he was wailing and mumbling about not having a home to go to, and being, 'quite unintelligent, he couldn't give us his personal details,' the report said. The railway police had tried to reason with him, by nicely suggesting that they needed to put the trains to bed, which only made him more anxious.

There was also a much younger man called Robert who was also on a train with a pile of books which he assembled across a whole row of seats and the other travellers complained. He said he didn't have anywhere to go, but that he was going to his friend Derrick's place, with the books, and that he'd fight anyone who might touch them, including the security guards. 'His speech was erratic and in answer to who he was, he said he found the question too simplistic and stupid,' the policeman had noted. 'This only raised my suspicions,' he added. The policeman also noted that Robert, 'went on and on about people saying he was disappearing down a bottomless pit of irony, which was a crazy thing to say.' After being detained Robert decided to voluntarily admit himself.

There was Johnny who had already been an in-mate of one of the regional prisons for disregarding all warnings about his manic snipping of gum trees. He was described as 'sullen and self righteous, and unable to see the error of his ways, and of fifty-two years of age'. He had been released after three months but was found illegally cutting down gum trees on a neighbour's property again, and the magistrate felt that he needed to be assessed as his behaviour was silently violent. And there was Julius, a relatively kind and thoughtful man in his late twenties who came from a town in the mid north after complaints from neighbours about his intense staring which frightened children. He was also caught shoplifting dog food at the local supermarket, even though it was known that he hardly ate anything himself.

Alice read through the entire file again and prepared herself to see them all together, given that they appeared to be introverted extroverts. Her phone rang several times and there was the usual early morning rush of emails from colleagues about next to nothing because people were anxiously trying to look important. She also had a brief chat with Margie, a close work colleague about what was troubling her in the file.

She drove to the hospital across the southern suburbs, past two giant malls where people were out and about doing their shopping and being self absorbed in socially approved ways. 'What secrets did they have,' she wondered. 'Would I ever find out if I initiated conversations with these strangers?'

She felt tired as her mother had had a bad fall, and the suggestion of a home for her was becoming more real by the day. She could recognize the first signs of an anxiety attack creeping into her head, but as a professional she called up her coping mechanisms, a wilful ability to concentrate on detail, and a talent for applying make up to any affected areas of the face.

The hospital was over sixty years old with interior features that seemed to mimic more homely places such as large upholstered armchairs and couches. There was also faux art and flowery paper on the walls and smiling doctors and nurses who were making an effort. To the side of the main building a fenced off annexe housed the seriously sick, who were being given high doses of medication.

She walked to the meeting room down a long corridor that was being mopped up by cleaners. Inside, in different chairs were the men she would interview, and glancing around she wondered what on earth it was she hoped to achieve. Everything about her job had become stressful as the waiting list of clients multiplied, and she was wondering how useful she could be given her on-going anxiety and the crazy world outside her files wouldn't stop for long enough for anyone to find peace.

Noticing how the men had arranged themselves around the room, yards apart, and that they were guarding their own space, she suggested that, 'we are going to have a talk about the reasons you are here.' They mumbled and protested, and in some cases, refused to take part, pointing out that they had already been taken there against their will. But after a few minutes, Walter was the first to speak. He was wiry, with a few earrings, and he seemed to her a frustrated idealist. He described himself as a musician.

*Well I'm here in the place they want to put me. It was a great idea to put up my sign on the back of the car, and for once people started talking, at least to me anyway. I was just too intense and the woman who complained about me has problems. At least I have loyalties – I'm not a criminal. Anyway, my story isn't some kind of naturalistic novel that'll make you feel better. The bastards, who put me in here, can't see the joke about sweet spots.*

He was clearly articulate and angry which could be a problem, Alice mused. 'People might think he was hiding something, but his sense of injustice might work against his need to relate to people outside,' she wrote in her notebook, knowing full well that she wouldn't express herself that way in her final reports.

The others nodded in agreement to what Walter had said, or at least with his vehement delivery, but William didn't seem to understand anything that was going on as he huddled in a corner near a heater, pleading to go home, that he was missing the train trips. But he managed a few lines. *Leave me alone – I need to get back on the trains. They are my trains.* He wouldn't say any more, instead he started to assemble himself into a ball on the floor.

Robert was very twitchy, his hands shook as he tried to speak and his head started to move from side to side. Alice had started making notes by this stage, in precise handwriting, evidence of someone who wanted to desperately shape order from mess, but she was thinking about her mother while he spoke. Robert spoke in raspy bursts, suggesting that he was always nervous.

*I try to be intellectually RESPONSIBLE!*

He stressed responsible with the look of a man who was imploding. *I want to know everything-put in everything – so I don't miss something – just like on my first day at uni – when I decided to read all the books on the ground floor as they were-um – more interesting than anything on the first-year course that the stupid lecturer wanted us to read. Anyway, I disagreed with him – I can't abide disagreement – I don't like people who don't agree with the subtle way I see things.*

Julius interjected against his better instincts. *Where is your landscape? Why can't you see a pattern to things?* But Robert just sat sullenly.

He looked like he was going to be sick, he was sweating and Alice noticed how frightened he was, and wondered what expectations had pushed him this far. By this time two ladies in white catering uniforms came in and delivered some scones and drinks, and they grabbed at them like monkeys in case they missed out as they were still getting used to the doleful menu of the hospital.

Julius was further energized after some food. *Why am I here? Yeah I lost it working in Canberra and driving across the country only made me worse. I always talk to myself, which seems strange to some people, no close relationships, a job that had ripped me apart – I wanted somewhere cosy, the car was like that on the trip, but it trapped me, cause all I could do was go on and on – there was nothing much when I got there. I have always been jealous of people who say they have a religious faith that explains everything and gives them a purpose.*

Alice intervened, 'were people friendly?'

*Friendly enough outside the cities cause we needed each other. I'm talking now because the town I ended up in gave me space and the animals loved me, but there really wasn't anything to do, and I didn't have any money. I can't remember the last time someone touched my hand. I'll go back if I can to the town as the Labrador George is pining according to Beryl at the animal shelter. But I need to be noticed and in the centre of things – but when I am, I can't cope – that's my problem Doctor, and I need a job.*

Alice was pleased that they were talking, even William in his own way, with his ability to say so much in a few words. She was though wondering how long it would go for as there were other appointments in her diary that afternoon, a needy procession of clients was waiting for her across the city, and with cutbacks in government spending, it was only getting worse, and she needed to call in on mum on her way home to see how she was going.

There was something else, the men, rather than having a conversation between each other, were talking to her, the female other, perhaps even the mother they never really knew, or the family they had always wanted. To some of her friends men were the oppressors, but this day in that room, such a view seemed like a catch cry, as none had jobs as such, and they were wards of the state. For some it meant they became violent, as so many traditional males, despite their huffing and puffing, lacked a language.

Across the city there were homeless men and women and along with unemployment there was declining dignity, the losers in Australia were largely out of sight, everyone, it seemed, was just another anonymous member of an amorphous middle class.

Johnny sat sullenly slightly apart from the rest of the group with his head almost in his lap. On occasions he had looked up when any of the others spoke, grumbling and snorting at some of their comments. In his case notes she noticed evidence of a violent family background, where there weren't any constructive role models plus details about cleverness at school and university, and that he, 'was a difficult character who refused to socialize', and that he, 'had a tendency towards dogmatism.'

Alice felt that if he contributed it would be a breakthrough as he was the only one who'd been in prison before and he might show a semblance of remorse as to why he was in there in the first place. Her notes suggested a compulsive disorder, but when did anything like that mesh into plain wilfulness or bastardry? He was tall and quite thin, and he gazed distractively at the others, but when something pricked his attention, he sat up and scribbled in a notebook and glared.

Alice confessed to herself, that, of the group, he was the one she didn't like very much, after chastising herself for such a personal reaction. She had also wandered off slightly in her thinking, as her mother had called her mobile during the break in garbled and disconsolate tones about an event in her street which seemed harmless, but which suggested a worrying level of decline.

Because Johnny wasn't volunteering, Alice suggested he talk about what led up to his incarceration. For a moment he glared at her, almost as if to say that she was being impudent and then he gradually gathered himself and stood up in the middle of the room. It looked like he was about to give a speech, or a performance, as he started to gyrate, waving his hands above his head and mouthing words. Eventually he started to speak,

*I know what's wrong with Australia more than any of you fools – it's simple, we are a dirty, dirty people with little idea of real class. You!*, he said, pointing at Walter, *run around with an idea that you can engage ordinary people who might find some dignity, but they are idiots who need putting in their place, cleaned up, and made to forget about being dignified. You see yourself as artistic, what a joke, the great philosophers and artists are all overseas, we just need to know our place, like those pesky gum trees that grow wherever they like. You see, I am part of an elite group.*

William was upset and started to cry without the words to come back at him, but he saw someone who, for some reason, hated himself. Alice was taken aback and flustered as it was something that responsible social work manuals suggested you keep well away from. Yet he was being honest, even if it was destructive, she rationalised.

Julius snorted, and briefly felt like hitting him in the head, but countered himself with the realization that it wouldn't be a good look during an assessment. He could see that he partly empathised, but only because he also felt powerless, the problem being that Johnny would never admit to that in front of anyone else.

But Johnny was on a roll and only warming up, Alice noted, debating with herself whether to terminate the meeting at that point. Before she could come to any conclusion, he was at it again.

*We need to keep this country as white as possible, clean in other words. When I was an archivist in the State Library, I refused to have anything to do with recording unpleasant accusations about so called massacres of aborigines on the west coast. There is no need for guilt – grief only makes us weak.*

*Have you ever spoken to anyone who has had sex with a black person? Some of the colour rubs off on your hands. I was jailed for doing my duty – if I had more time I would have a go at herding up the aborigines in those outback settlements and making them have a wash – but you probably wouldn't know if they'd got any cleaner because they are so dark. We are also being invaded by other dark people who aren't from civilized continents like Europe.*

Everyone gasped in their own way as Johnny's statement was too feral to be contained within any idea of camaraderie, that they were all there together, and should support one another.

Robert, who had hardly said anything, and seemed to be in a

permanent spiral of self doubt, was even motivated to speak up as he tried not to hear the nihilism in his head and the violence of political figures around the second world war of whom he had read, but his delivery was stymied by apologetic stuttering, and his words were no match. He dissembled,

*Um – aren't you being reductive? It's not philosophically tenable to have such simple opinions, but maybe I haven't read as much as you.*

Alice had lost control for maybe the same reasons as her country, which wasn't confident enough to assert itself over the bluster and innuendo hiding inside the shell of its soul.

She decided to terminate the meeting, to the relief of the participants, except for Johnny who said he was being censored and cut short. Maybe he had a last rhetorical flourish to perform, Alice wondered, but she didn't really care less, and she was worried about her mum, and her other appointments that day. She would also have to write up her case notes and recommendations later. Except for Johnny, they silently filed out of the room to return to their wards and, as if nothing had happened, the catering staff returned to clear up the used dishes and carry away the coffee machine.

As much as it was possible, she started thinking about her report, but driving out of the car park she reminded herself she needed to see her mum on the way home. Her last appointments were quite easy compared to her 'meeting' with the men at Bayside. Her mother lived in a nondescript street in one of the southern suburbs, the residents had backyards and leafy gardens, and it was possible to live quietly without the neighbours knowing about illness or disaster. Driving into Shelbourne Avenue, memories of childhood flooded her, such as the time when mum took her to the park for the first time, the slight hill down from where she and her sister rode their bikes, and the vacant block where Mr Benson kept a horse, and a sheep that kept the grass under control.

Her mother was in a state, mumbling disconcertedly about an event in the neighbourhood that day, shaking and pacing. She said that it was a nasty incident, an intruder had come across the back fence next door, but that she couldn't remember her neighbour's name, and she even struggled to recall that of her late husband. Then she started to cry. Alice knew it wouldn't be long before people from the council would be called in to look after her, and even that would only be a temporary measure. Alice tried to calm her and made a few discreet calls on her mobile, hoping that her mother wouldn't overhear.

Driving home was one of those journeys most people have at one time or another in their lives; the world was fuzzy, she was numb, and scenarios crowded into her, and so she was careful to pay close attention to the road ahead.

In the morning she had to try to make sense of her notes from the meeting. She had no appointments away from the office and going to work on the train there were people who looked like the strange and intensely human men of the day before, but these were quiet and courteous, even if withdrawn. The railway station was where all these individuals exited, maybe met up with other people and then disappeared. Her office wasn't all that far away and her short-prescribed route took her past the familiar faces of the homeless who crowded into a laneway between McDonalds and a rundown sex shop off one of the main boulevards.

She tried to assemble the notes into a coherent pile, disregarding the many asides, and some quite artistic doodles, she had scribbled onto government notepaper. There were the legal documents from the magistrates' court detailing that the clients could be considered a danger either to themselves or others. Robert though was aware that he wasn't coping and had admitted himself.

She finally organized the information into discrete piles highlighted by yellow post it notes and gathered her thoughts for the recommendations she would make. She saw Margie in the corridor and had a reassuring chat with her about her feelings, and whether they were useful in the circumstances. Margie, as a mother of three, was sensible, she always thought, and she relied on her in such times. Margie said, 'just try to clear your head', after which Alice returned to her assessments.

It was obvious that, 'everyone except for Johnny suffers from ailments that couldn't be considered dangerous', she wrote. 'Each of these men is obsessive in varying degrees, some of which might be treated with moderate doses of drugs, and by large amounts of love, and more connection to society after a more thorough investigation of their individual circumstances.' Privately, she said to herself that they could of course be saner than the rest of us. She paused, and knew of course, how it was that they had got to see her in the first place, and that she was editorializing. That she was involved in ways she never imagined she would be, but that was ok, as a statement needed to be made somewhere, even if much of what she wrote, and would write, wouldn't appear in the official case notes.

Of Robert and Johnny it was never that simple. 'Robert it seems is strangely happy being isolated, and sadly special, because so much is happening in his head he fears freedom. 'I recommend that a psychiatrist assess him.' Such was the nature of the process she was caught up in that her hand quivered when she wrote that, because like many of the post seventies generation, Alice wanted the world to be a nicer place (and she tried hard to play her part in improving it), even when she saw how grotesque it could be.

So, when faced with Johnny, all motherhood statements and best intentions, were challenged as she wanted to be seen, in the face of her friends, as caring and considerate, and never unkind.

'Johnny, although his snipping of gum trees has resulted in a criminal conviction, and isn't strictly violence against other people, is, I believe, capable of extreme violence. His activities, to this stage, have largely been symbolic, but never benign.' She was aware again that she was perhaps stepping across the boundaries of her brief.

She continued, 'the extent to which his actions are conditioned by underlying social structures and his opposition to them should be taken into consideration, but I believe that he should be retained and treated, at least for his own good. His need to destroy that which he loves is hand in hand with psychotic behaviour manifesting itself in covert extreme politics at this stage, some of which we have seen before in anxious times. Hopefully, he can be redeemed by unexpected love, but in the meantime, I fear that that none of us will be safe unless this action is taken.'

www.ingramcontent.com/pod-product-compliance
Ingram Content Group Australia Pty Ltd
76 Discovery Rd, Dandenong South VIC 3175, AU
AUHW020135130726
429791AU00003B/122

9 781925 801200